Abundance of the Infinite

Abundance of the Infinite

Christopher Canniff

QUATTRO BOOKS

The publication of *Abundance of the Infinite* has been generously supported by the Canada Council for the Arts and the Ontario Arts Council.

Cover design: Sean Poling
Editor: Luciano Iacobelli
Typography: Grey Wolf Typography

Library and Archives Canada Cataloguing in Publication

Canniff, Christopher
    Abundance of the infinite / Christopher Canniff.

Issued also in an electronic format.

ISBN 978-1-927443-07-1

I. Title.

PS8605.A574A78 2012   C813'.6   C2012-903892-X

Published by Quattro Books Inc.
382 College Street
Toronto, Ontario, M5T 1S8
www.quattrobooks.ca

Printed in Canada

What is man ... Doesn't he lack power just when he needs it most? Whether he is uplifted by joy or engulfed by suffering, is he not stopped in both conditions and brought back to dull, cold consciousness just when he is ready to lose himself in the abundance of the infinite?

– Goethe

1

YELENA AND HER DOCTOR had terrible news. The ultrasound and the blood test done at eleven weeks had revealed both Down syndrome and a possible heart defect in the fetus. More conclusive testing could be done, but the results were fairly certain. Atypical cell division in either the sperm or the egg meant this was either my fault or hers, our individual culpability impossible to discern. The child, a girl, would have some degree of mental retardation, the possibility of childhood leukemia, and the possibility of abnormalities in the immune and gastrointestinal systems, dementia, and seizures. She would develop a flattened face, a small head and a short neck. A team of professionals would be required, among them a pediatric cardiologist, a developmental pediatrician, physical and occupational therapists and neurologists. All of this, as explained by the doctor and through subsequent research, for a child which, with Yelena over forty years old and both of us only one year into our marriage, was unplanned. Yelena declared that she might want the pregnancy terminated as her doctor has encouraged her to do.

This announcement came on the same day that my mother called to inform me of what should have been, by comparison, the almost inconsequential news that my father, who I had not seen since I was a child, has died of cancer in Ecuador—a pronouncement that made me feel more of a sense of loss than I should have, and more than I imagined I was capable of feeling for this man who I have not seen in decades, who abandoned me from an early age and who left my mother early on in their marriage before the onset of her constant drinking, for reasons largely unknown to my mother and, by extension, myself.

"Giving a child up for adoption is easy," I explain one evening during a candle-lit dinner of *confit de canard*, roasted potatoes with garlic, and dark Pommard wine—a wine Yelena drank, but as I do not drink, I never touch, a wine smelling fruity and floral and, she says, tasting of minerals that are heady on the tongue. I have no experience with adoption and therefore have no justification to make my claim. Additionally, I could never imagine myself giving my child away to anyone. But still, I am of the opinion that I need to convince her of its veracity in order to see our child born into the world.

She looks down and shakes her head sullenly. "I will become too attached," she says in her characteristically slow and strained, but still forceful, Russian-inflected English. Lowering her fork onto her plate, she adds: "I will not be able to just hand it over to a stranger when it's born."

"That doesn't make any sense," I reply, without explaining the obvious contradiction between this statement and the announcement she had made earlier. "Let yourself be attached to it."

At that moment, I realize that the last sentence she spoke was uttered with an odd, even slightly vigorous conviction.

I plead further but she will not listen, choosing instead to rationalize and justify, finishing her wine and then rolling the dark stained cork around on the table as she alludes to the mediocre and inferior life the child will have, and the burden the child will place upon us for the duration of our lives. She speaks of the special schools in which the child will need to be enrolled, and the ongoing cost of institutions once the child becomes an adult. She feels pressured by her doctor to decide now, in order to avoid medical risks that he said will be associated with a late termination.

"But still," Yelena says, perhaps sensing the desperation in my facial expressions and in my voice, despite my attempts at concealing my apprehension, and perhaps because of my earlier assertion that I want to attend my father's burial in Ecuador, "whatever my doctor says, maybe I can hold off the decision for a short time."

Although she has given me reason not to trust her before—going after another man she met at her library job after agreeing to marry me, returning the engagement ring and then coming back when the other man left—this time is different. There was a certain tone of maternal defiance in her voice when she declared how she would not give her child to a stranger at an adoption agency; and, if she would not, then it could be extrapolated that she would not provide the fetus to a doctor whose intent was prenatal homicide, especially when she had promised her husband to postpone any such resolution. And as my consolation has always been to run, to escape from inexorable circumstances and to thereby flee the source of my own obsessive thoughts, my anxiety, my panic attacks and tormenting dreams, attending my father's burial in Ecuador seems not only logical but rational. I additionally conclude that if I am not here, she cannot convince me of anything other than that to which we have already agreed.

∞

I stand before the sprawling office window of my clinical psychology practice at dusk, high above the Toronto city streets. The noises of buses and car tires resound on the street below. A news truck is parked nearby. The coppery image on an adjacent building's mirrored glass oscillates between reflections of melting ice and the unsteady wavering of skaters whose blades will soon turn to wheels crushing the discarded flower petals of spring. The lake a hundred metres away is flecked with ice, moving steadily on: white-grey corpuscles of static water parading beneath the nylon flapping of a Canadian flag.

As I see these images beneath the sky's pink and blue-grey hues of sunset, I think of the way Yelena kissed me for the last time in the back of a taxicab, the windows rolled down as I brought her home after our final dinner together, consumed at our favourite restaurant nestled between narrow buildings in a brick back alley in Little Italy. She kissed me forcibly, abruptly, with an artful passion somehow obscure in meaning. The baby seemed to be all we talked about when we were together, but on that night we had no such discussions, and the touch of her moist lips, the smell of jasmine and patchouli oil on her skin, and the brisk evening air all seemed to exude consent at the conferred recognition that the time we would spend apart was not only necessary, but would be somehow beneficial.

"Do not stay away long," Yelena said into my ear, softly, abruptly adding after a time: "Love cannot last in a void." The tinge of her voice was foreboding, at the same time formal, as though she was at a wedding, reading from a variation on First Corinthians at a church podium. She continued speaking, if not in actuality, at least in my remembrance of that moment: "Love can never perpetuate in absence, except in our unreliable memories, memories that capture short spans of time and later distort them."

Memories of her expressions, facial features and physical touches in those instants, I knew, would remain with me intact. I can still feel her ghostly fingers wrapped around mine, their curvature and moisture still retained in my mind. I expected her to say goodbye, but instead, our hands locked in a sweaty and tired embrace, she said that she missed me already.

Before leaving, she made a gesture that startled and surprised me. The gesture—a simple motion of her hand away from mine, minutes before she stepped toward the front door of our house, which was, for now, temporarily hers—seemed perhaps her way of alleviating any indebtedness she felt toward the promise she had made.

I stay in my office for a few days, referring any patients who call to a colleague, my own therapist named Richard with whom I maintain contact, all the time contemplating whether I should return to the house and ask Yelena if the motion of her hand in the cab was, in fact, a release from her obligation to me. But then, I finally conclude that she would think me obsessing again, such a statement being the manifestation of days of worthless fixation on a meaningless action, Richard having convinced me that she would be right. And so I go nowhere, gathering a few of my belongings together into a backpack and stopping frequently to watch the street below.

My separation from Yelena and our unborn child, and the news of my father who I should have by all means forgotten, smells of Bombay Gin, imbibed by a man who professes not to drink, and chana masala, butter chicken and tapas, spiced olives, spicy potatoes, garlic shrimp and ham croquettes, all consumed as I watch dull depictions of random architecture and wandering Toronto crowds seeming like sad people living workaday lives.

I try not to think about Yelena, our unborn daughter I had tentatively named Annabelle, my father's neglect, or about love, regret, or indebtedness as I purchase a ticket to return to Manta, a small coastal fishing town in Ecuador.

I visited my father in Manta a few times when I was a child, in the place he lived for almost forty years before his death. I have only been to Ecuador and briefly to Spain. I've always had the longing to move out into the world so I could travel and see more of what different cultures and histories and natural environments have to offer. But apart from Spain, because of my lifelong desire to see that country, I've simply never known where else I should go. I sit down and write a letter to Yelena, a letter detailing how long I will stay, a month, perhaps two, and the reason why, so she can have the time to contemplate the irrationality of wanting an end to our daughter's life.

Richard encourages me to go, with the caveat that I keep a dream journal and a daily account of my life while I am away. I tell him I will.

Yelena calls the next day, after receiving my letter, angrily telling me not to go without giving a reason, as if we had never previously discussed my impending departure, calling my decision to leave both foolish and irresponsible. She leaves me incensed messages on my answering machine when I am out, or when I let the phone ring. When I do not return her calls for several days, the anger in her messages gradually turns to irritation, mild annoyance, and then finally to acceptance. She sends me a letter urging me to go and I finally pick up the phone. Many of our last conversations are at three or four o'clock in the morning, when her calls awaken me from a tumultuous slumber. Saying she cannot sleep either, she begins repeating some of the same advice I have given her over the past years I have known her, given before she went on trips to Europe where she met various friends and cousins, aunts and uncles. As I was doling out that largely pragmatic advice—not only where to visit based upon my research into these areas, but also what she might expect based upon who she would be seeing, and how she could open herself up to the benefit of that experience (whether the gain was through suffering or through joy)—I thought she wasn't listening. But I suppose now that I was wrong.

In a recurring nightmare I have over the next few days, the type that, as a psychologist, I understand is due to my repeatedly missing the unconscious meaning of the dream, Yelena stands in a closet. I can't see her, but I know she is there. There is nothing more I can ever recall about this dream, even when I make the conscious choice before I fall asleep to remember all of its details.

When I awaken, sitting up, sweating, hyperventilating and struggling to catch my breath, I have an image of the closed closet door, and the remembrance that she was inside. She is not claustrophobic, so it is not a dream about her fear, although it is rooted in my own. The dream has no direct literal meaning. Freud tells me this may be an allusion to her life; not what it is to her, but what my subconscious mind perceives of it. She is closeted in. Trapped. But dreams, once dissected, often have the opposite meaning. Yelena is predictably linked, in my waking life, to my fear for Annabelle's life. I may have projected my own feelings onto Yelena and, in so doing, may be the one who is trapped inside that closet because of my regret over leaving her and Annabelle behind. Still, despite this apparent understanding, my subconscious will not let these visions and their associated thoughts go, and I continue to experience this dream.

I think of how ridiculous and devious my subconscious mind is. My dreams—while often a source of pain, once analyzed, and a stream of never-ending absurdity while engulfed in them—have always, especially now, been preferable to the futility and derisiveness of what encompasses and overwhelms my subconscious thoughts by day.

∞

I sit drinking another contemptible Bombay Gin and tonic alone in my office, unable to sleep, looking out over the city streets at night with the sounds of reveling below. Certain that any attempt at sleep will result in the same recurring nightmare with accompanying thoughts of Yelena and Annabelle and, upon awakening, my father, I write a note to Richard. In the letter I detail, in my exhaustion, the thoughts I have of my father—that, although he was not present throughout my childhood, the few visits I had to Ecuador to see him had a profound psychological effect. I was no longer the abandoned child but one interacting with his unknown father, who seemed, at least when we were together, to be kind and even somewhat loving toward me, which made our subsequent separation even more difficult and somehow, in my childish mind, unjustified.

I finally fall asleep on the couch and awaken just after midnight as if from a nightmare, rising suddenly, violently, falling not down but upwards, and I sit up straight with a panic accompanied by a sudden, intense moment of overwhelming terror. I try not to move but I tremble, locked in sweat, my chest and throat tight, adrenaline flowing through me, unable to catch my breath as though I have been running long and hard. I walk into the washroom and splash water on my face before I lie back down again. I am winded and exhausted but a long time passes as I attempt to calm myself, staring at the nighttime ceiling like Proust as a boy lying at his Aunt Leonie's home in Illiers, France in his insomnia. I frantically try to forget my fear borne of a nightmare I have not had, a nightmare that I certainly would have recollected had I woken so suddenly in the midst of it, a nightmare supplanted by what must be the worst nocturnal panic attack I've ever experienced. In the folds and crevices of the stucco ceiling I can see the light from the street flickering off of the uneven surface, shadows wavering and forming into different shapes and memories. I struggle to close my eyes so that I will not see any of this, trying now to think of whatever will relax me, getting up to open the windows outside the office and listening to the people drunkenly roaming the streets below, howling and singing.

As I listen to their hideous caterwauling I think of nothing but the rhythm of the perpetually cleansing and undulating sea of the place I am going to, before I am finally able, after what must be hours, to fall into sleep again....

2

IN MY SLEEP DEPRIVATION I sit among vast, uncluttered fields and forests leading down to a winding river. Lush greenery, rolling hills and cliffs are in every direction, and all of this is illuminated by a cloudless sky. I am suddenly overcome by an overwhelming serenity and a sense of incredible peace as I find myself in the netherworld between reality and dreams....

There is a thunderous noise, and I quickly awaken from my trance.

A child has fallen to the floor of the bus beside me, and he has begun to cry. His mother, a young woman with darkened skin and wearing a multicolored shawl, runs over and collects him. My mind re-acclimates to my surroundings, to the sound of subdued trumpets, un-tuned guitars and melodic voices. The slow-paced salsa music from the bus's tinny speakers mixes with the raucous noise of the child's howls. Looking out of the window I see a sheer cliff next to the bus, a precipice that snakes through windy hills that extend a hundred feet down to a river in the valley below.

Looking down over the cliff's edge as we meander along the dirt road at an excessive rate of speed, the loud and ever-changing rhythms of the music seeming to encourage the driver to take us faster, then slower, then faster again, I think of the periodic news reports I have heard about buses in Peru careening over the edge of a mountain, the buses filled to capacity, and I suddenly recall Yelena's fear of dying alone. Ironically, in addition to that worry was Yelena's admission that she loved loneliness. It was the only feeling she claimed she could control. She had learned how to be in a state of loneliness at any time she chose, even when surrounded by people on the subway or in a streetcar, conditioning herself to such a meditative temperament by hearing, or even remembering, a certain song that she had once associated with a period of solitary and secluded time in her life, or a specific passage of a book, the transcribed thoughts of Pessoa, Kafka, Bulgakov or Dostoevsky, or a simple reminiscence, either of which could bring her to what she referred to as a state of solitary euphoria. She treasured the feeling of loneliness because that is what she claimed she was best at: feeling lonely.

And this was one of the first traits I found that we had in common.

Falling into a trance again, peering out of the windows of the bus, thinking of my past and the last time I was here decades ago, alone, I suddenly feel cognizant of, and comfortable in, my solitude.

Rejecting dream symbolism and dream dictionaries, where compiled lists can indicate the significance of a dream (knowing, of course, that dream images only hold significance insofar as what they represent to the conscious self, as any Jungian can attest), I rebuff the knowledge that the start of a journey in dreams symbolizes death. If I did believe in such symbolism, I would have instead chosen to embrace the dream symbol of water, in the valley below, as life.

The last thought I recall as I fall asleep, dreaming of a long, winding river with innumerable tributaries, is how the river water will soon transform to the water of the ocean once I again locate the place in which my father lived, his apartment that overlooked the sea. I wonder what emotion, if any, I will see in his reticent face....

∞

"*Hola, señor*," a man says to me as I step off the bus, still drowsy with sleep. "Welcome to Manta."

He is short with sun-ripened skin, and stands beside a weathered taxi cab on a dirty street. I am certain I have seen him before. I suddenly realize that I haven't spoken to anyone in days, apart from hotel clerks who seemed suspicious of me somehow, and hefty bus drivers who spoke no English and could only communicate through the names of various towns and cities, mocking my pronunciation of them.

Being here again I feel as though I am a child once more, untroubled and carefree, as though my father is still alive and we can play on the beach and bury each other in sand, walking along the same wide expanses early in the morning to meet the fishermen with the freshest fish, some of the fish long, slender and dark, with rows of sharp teeth, and we can sit and eat *ceviche*, cold fish soup, in restaurants along with bottles of exceptionally sweet-tasting Coca-Cola, and *encebollado*, warm fish soup sold out of the sides of houses, and we can read novels together on his apartment patio and spend long nights at the parties on the beach, drinking more Coca-Cola as he imbibes *cerveza* after *cerveza*, listening without a care to music and watching as the people dance barefoot in the sand. I have reverted to my own youthful and jovial self.

But still, not all is how I remember it.

"Why is it so dusty here?" I ask the man before me.

"Ah, *polvo*, yes," he says, kicking at the dirt road. "It is the dry season."

He extends his hand upward, and looks to the sky. "No rain," he continues. "We here are too poor. We can only afford two seasons, wet and dry. Not like your country."

He smiles widely, revealing some missing teeth.

"*Maletas*, your bags?" he asks, eyeing my backpack.

"I have no bags," I say.

He looks confused. I am not a local, and yet I have brought no luggage. I do not feel the need to explain that my only possessions are all contained in my small backpack: a few changes of clothes and some toiletries, some books—an English-Spanish dictionary and a copy of Boccaccio's *The Decameron* among them—a picture of Yelena and her last letter to me, an ultrasound photograph of Annabelle, my tear-resistant 'do not disturb' sign for my door, pens, some writing paper and a journal, a flashlight, a passport, and a roll of money bound with an elastic band.

As I walk away from the taxis and the bus station, past the marina and outdoor patios with plastic chairs and the smell of grilled shrimp and fish, I see an inlet in the distance.

A single boat sits atop stilts. It must be low tide because there is a group of fishing boats lying on their sides on the muddy ground beside it. This boat constructed over a wooden frame is the only one still upright, perhaps usable only as a house. I recall how high and low tides are affected by the moon, and how I might walk by here tomorrow and see that all of these boats are floating, and that the water covering this house-boat's stilts makes it appear as though it, too, is buoyant. A man and his family emerge from the hold of the house-boat and rise up to the deck. One of the children, his spindly arm high in the air, waves to me. I am a stranger here—a tourist, a *gringo*—which, judging by the appearance of this place and the stares I am noticing, they do not see often. I walk on. Sauntering past rows of palm trees, I proceed down to the beach. There is lemonade here and salted, unripe mangos for sale. There is music, soft and sweet. I run toward the water, dropping my backpack behind me, removing my shirt and tossing it into the sand, and I look up from a line of distant fishing boats to see the daytime moon. As I rush toward what I imagine to be the sweet sticky smell of the water, the moon seems exceptionally bright. I feel the soft sweet salt caressing my face, and the cool waves splashing against me.

I have never felt such exquisite and invigorating water as this, and I instantly recall that in my childhood, the few times I was here, I was free to jump straight into this same ocean as my father stood on the beach playing his bagpipes onshore, the muted, complex *legato*—wailing emanating from the expanded sheepskin bag surrounding me as my body was immersed in warm water, the depths from which I imagined I would be content never to emerge.

Here I can see the riches of Atahualpa, the ancient Incan emperor held captive by the Spanish Conquistadors for months before being executed by them, in every drop of water splashing against my chest and reflecting back into the sea. The largest ransom ever paid, tons of silver, gold and gems from all over the country of Peru, is now paying reverence to my presence here in the form of tiny crystals and prized stones. These thoughts are not logical, I tell myself. My life until now has been built and lived on logic and deductive reasoning. I have never imagined Atahualpa's ransom before when stepping out of the shower, tiny droplets of gold and silver beside the drain and on the walls and floor of the shower flecked with his blood.

These rolling, liberating waves that turn over themselves without ceasing whirl through the day that transforms itself into night.

3

I AWAKEN TO THE sound of dogs growling on the street outside my *hosteleria* in Manta, a very small hotel with only three rooms. It is midnight. Tomorrow, I will go to the place where my father lived. A man and a woman are arguing loudly, in Spanish, in the hallway. Tap water is drumming incessantly on the bottom of my bathroom sink. Yelena's last letter to me is open on the table, which is beside my thin mattress and outside the mosquito netting of the bed. I am sweating. Is this part of a dream? I can hear Yelena's voice as I retrieve the letter and begin reading it with my flashlight:

"... I am too cowardly, and you are too brave. I watch the clouds and see hideous dragons where you see them turning into butterflies ... you see beauty in everything ... you see life as a gift, not to be wasted ... you are like Dostoevsky's dreamer, and I am his Nastenka—while I cling wholeheartedly to my home, my grandmother and the lodger, you perceive—in Dostoevsky's words—one moment of bliss as sufficient for your entire life ... you need no one...."

I put the letter down, and her voice stops. Is she right? Do I need no one? The indisputable proof of her assertion might be my presence here, alone, in a country virtually unknown to me, in a place a thousand miles from my home, in a corner of the world I have never truly known. Is she trying to convince me that, in fact, I need no one, herself and Annabelle included, and that I can feel guiltless for leaving them by setting this idea in my mind, distracting me by her subtlety, placing the last phrase inconspicuously, almost as an afterthought, while first presenting a more compelling, poignant and thoughtful image? She is wrong about me seeing beauty in everything, and seeing life as a gift. I have seen her blindly and unjustifiably attributing such noble traits before, projecting characteristics she perhaps wished she possessed herself upon others.

The argument in the hall is growing louder.

I get up and place my privacy sign on the outside of my door, thinking I will need to make this habitual, watching as a man in shorts and a woman in a small, thin gown in the hallway look over at me, surprised, and stop shouting their incoherent phrases. I want to explain to them that Samuel Taylor Coleridge once claimed to have dreamed the entire narrative of "Kubla Khan" and that, after a tumult of frenzied writing, he was then interrupted by a knock on the door and was later able to transcribe only a portion of the remainder of the dream. My therapist Richard requires that I keep a very detailed dream journal, I would explain, so such a disgrace must never happen to me. The man and woman, still staring at me, immediately return to their room together, slamming the door behind them, and their now muted dialogue continues and echoes through the hall, the reverberation of their voices eventually dissipating.

∞

Guilt may often be a substitute for other emotions, but in my case, for what?

My dreams that night are rapid and confused. This is too early in my journey, my mind too disorderly and cluttered for my dreams to be coherent. Immediately upon awakening to silence and darkness, the only illumination a fragment of moonlight from under the curtains and the only noise from a chorus of crickets and the terrible, interminable ticking of tapwater droplets on the bottom of my sink, I remember an anchor point by which I can recall the remainder of this dream. Retrieving my journal, a pen and my flashlight, I write about the flag and the currency depicting the independence of this country born of Simón Bolivar. I recollect and transcribe that, earlier in the dream, I could see the Spanish Colonies, with the King of Spain's spies looking for the reasons why the colonies are not producing. There were whisperings of corruption and I recall more now, going further back in time, back to Pizzaro and Almagro, the two groups of the Spanish who arrived to decimate the Incans through disease, overwork and war, who arrived to indoctrinate their religion without perhaps seeing a future of holocaust but nonetheless providing the proper conditions for it. As I see those groaning and pleading for my help, knowing somehow that I am a doctor who is cognizant of their thoughts, I explain that I am not a medical doctor but a psychologist; one who knows nothing of how to solve such immense problems, but who can only show them the world of their minds, and mostly in theory proven through sometimes sparse and dubious case studies..."I can do nothing for you," I say, "I am powerless here...."

4

I HAVE THE CHARACTERISTIC symptoms: distorted vision and surreal sensations, my fingers and hands tingling and appearing to grow longer as I walk toward the front door of the apartment building I have come to know through visits to my father. I have not been here since long before my father's death, and my trembling and the sense of terror I have about a need to escape, losing control, a powerlessness in the face of what I am about to experience, is palpable. I shiver as pains in my chest worsen, and I am reminded of the intensity of my recent nocturnal panic attack. I have the intuition that whoever answers the door will tell me that my father has just died. I know, I will say, that is why I am here. Whoever answers will escort me to my father's lifeless body, and I will see in my father's closed eyes only distant and faded memories. Knocking on that door will startle me into a state of anxiety in which I will lose control, lashing out insolently at whoever stands before me.

In my psychology practice, I have helped those with such anxiety by utilizing various techniques for relaxation, while gradually increasing their exposure to the situations which initially caused their apprehension and angst. For me, from an early age, standing before closed doors through which I have no access has always caused me to experience a sense of powerlessness and panic, and although I often stand for long durations in front of locked doors for this reason, until now, this effort, along with varied breathing exercises, has been to no avail.

I have traced the root of my nervousness back, along with my therapist, to when I was here to visit my father as a young child of twelve or thirteen. I had arrived upstairs, in front of the door on which I had always knocked, only no one was there. I discovered later that my father was at the beach and had simply forgotten the time. But in the duration between when I had first knocked on the door and when I had finally resorted in frustration to aimlessly wandering the streets, later roaming across the wide beaches, I had knocked louder, and then pounded and pounded on that door, cursing and detesting that door for being closed and locked, slinking down to the base of the painted metal and crying as though he had died, longing to smash one of the windows infuriatingly barred to prevent unwanted entry, shifting my backpack up over my shoulder, wanting to do anything to get inside, to bring him back to life.

I arrive at this front door now, sweating, my fingers numb, shifting the backpack, which has slipped, back over my shoulder. This heavy, white painted metal, windowless door that drags on the floor under its own weight when opened has not changed since my arrival here when I was twelve or thirteen. There is not even a different colour of paint, or a plant beside it now, or any sort of decorative border. All is the same. My mouth is dry and I feel myself lifting my hand, my movements slow, my mind longing to convalesce to its normal state, and I am fighting against the sensation of heaviness in my hand with the longing to pound at this door with my closed fist, to combat this door and to fight my way inside so that my father might somehow still be alive. I also have the sudden urge to escape, though, to run away from this place and to regain control of my heart's rapid pulse, to relinquish the dizziness and nausea, to wander the streets again as though I am a child, crying and crying and calling out, over and over again, for my father.

I knock once, then twice, then again, lightheaded now, and as I prepare to slink away, a woman opens the door leading into her oceanfront apartment. My anxiety, fears and pain subside at the sight of her. It is Señora Modesta, my self-professed "Ecuadorian mother," who is shorter than I remember. She has the same round belly and the same wet towel draped over her apron that I recall, the towel the same as her right hand, covered in paint. I am much taller than her now.

I have the impression, from the scowl on her face, that she is suspicious of me as a stranger; for a moment, somehow, she does not seem to recognize me. She has not seen me, or perhaps any strangers, for decades. She looks confused, and as she holds on to the door, I wonder if she is preparing to force it shut. I clench my fist and notice the smell of frying plantains and baking fish from within. I feel my anxiety returning and, along with it, my desire to flee.

"Samuel!" she suddenly says with a smile, startling me. I am unaccustomed to hearing the Spanish pronunciation of my name and the associated accentuation of the final consonant.

Without waiting for a response, she wipes her hand with the towel, and then uses a cloth to wipe paint from the door handle. She still manages to keep her left hand on the door.

"*Buenos dias, Señora Modesta*," I say.

She grabs my face with both hands, kissing each of my cheeks which are now burning.

"I am sorry for your father," she says, her smile transforming into a frown. "We have not seen you for so long. You have grown into a man...."

Then, after a moment, there is a woman's voice from inside. "*Mami*, who is it?"

"Enter, enter," the Señora says to me, and I feel my disquiet, frustration and panic slowly beginning to drift away again.

She struggles to pull the door open, and she invites me inside. Two women, distinctly beautiful, one with long, dark brown hair, and the other with short, black hair, both of them slender and wearing form-fitting and colourful clothing, are sitting at the table, smiling.

"Samuel, you remember my daughters Inés and Yolanda," the Señora says.

"The last time I saw them, they were babies," I reply.

They take immediate notice and begin staring at me, at my freckles, ruddy cheeks and red hair that are so different from anyone else's appearance here. They rise and we exchange kisses.

The smell of fish and plantains frying in oil is strong now. There is also another odour lingering here, not quite as strong: the smell of new paint.

The Señora urges me to be seated and I pull out a chair, set my backpack on the ground, and sit down. As I do, her daughters rise from their seats and hurry to pile rice, cheese, breaded fish and oily plantains on a plate, handing the steaming food to their mother.

"*Aquí está*," she says, placing the full plate before me. She pours a small glass of juice, which looks freshly blended, and a cup of instant coffee. After putting them on the table in front of me, she sits down.

"*Gracias, Señora*," I say.

As I eat, I look around to see that her apartment is the same as I remember, small but seemingly comfortable. Their dog is barking behind the wooden door at the back. There are painted statues of various sizes, among them a large number of statues of saints I don't recognize. There are statues of the Virgin Mary, statues of dogs, a black cat, even a dragon. The Señora notices that I have taken an interest in them. She reaches over, retrieves a statue and hands it to me.

"St. Francis of Assisi," she says, the half-completed statue wetting my fingers with paint. I hand it back to her, and wipe my fingers on the edge of my plate.

"I like paint," she says in English.

"You like *to* paint," I say.

"I like *to* paint," she repeats, smiling as she amends her words. "My daughters must to learn English. Your father taught me, but not them."

"I would also like to learn," I say, uncomfortable, nervous somehow. "Not to paint sculptures, but canvases. To capture the essence of a moment so it won't be forgotten. Much like telling yourself, before you fall asleep, that you will remember your dreams. I went to Madrid, and the art there inspired me to want to create my own unique impressions of what I see around me." I can tell she is confused by my words, and I feel as though I am rambling. "Perhaps one day," I add, "I will learn to paint." She nods, seeming to understand this.

She produces a small slip of paper, handing it to me for my perusal as she places the statue down on the table. The words are typewritten in Spanish. Before I can explain that I do not understand, she turns the paper over in my hand. The back side is written in English:

> *He who works with his hands is a labourer.*
> *He who works with his hands and his head is a craftsman.*
> *He who works with his hands and his head and his heart*
>   *is an artist.*
> *St. Francis of Assisi (b. 1181).*

"*Bello*," I say.

The Señora replaces the statue and the paper, and turns back toward me.

"Your father, he will be buried tomorrow," she says. "At noon. We are all sorry here, that he has died. He was a good man to us ... and so, where are you staying? How long are you in Manta?"

"I was staying at a *hosteleria* nearby. Now, if you have an apartment available, perhaps I will stay here."

As I continue eating, I struggle through casual conversation. The Señora and her daughters speak in their native tongue quickly, much faster on the coast than in the Andes mountains. I cannot comprehend their words, or even hope to converse with them. I long to explain to the Señora, who would appreciate such sentiments, how much I learned from and was inspired by the art in Madrid, specifically at the Museo del Prado, where I saw the enduring art of the ages. I would tell her that I have found it is comprised, much like Tolstoy concluded in his book *What is Art?*, mostly of religious works.

I would disregard the therapeutic benefits of painting, as touted by Richard, and would explain further, knowing that she has likely never been to Spain, that the works in the Museo del Prado are composed of primitive Italian art; a divine light represented in leafs of gold, with man in the background showing his smallness as per the medieval emphasis on God. A pregnant Virgin whose praying hands are perched atop her round belly is captured in the precise centre of one of the paintings, the tree of life on the bottom left, twenty-two pairs of hands with awed faces devoutly praying to the belly. The Christ Child is atop the throned Virgin Mary. His head is perfect in every aspect, His hands, the glow about His face, the soft curls of His hair represented in exacting detail. Saint John the Baptist is in the desert with falcons and lizards and many-eyed sheep. The snake of Genesis is there, as is Saint Francis protruding from a ring of flowers and fruit. Saint Michael stands frozen while battling the fallen angels. The archangel Gabriel in fitted armour is engulfed by spectators while kicking an angel with the heel of his foot and stabbing at Golgotha with a shining sword. Horrified people on boats are bound for the fiery lakes of eternal damnation. The martyrdom of Saint Sebastian, whose body, full of arrows, supports an anguished head, is depicted. Saint Helen sits atop a dark horse at the gates of Jerusalem, along with a gloomy entourage. The emperor Heracles is astride another dark horse, observed from above by a glowing angel as he carries a wooden cross. Santo Domingo of Silos and the Spanish King Ferdinand are meeting outside of castle walls. A repentant Saint Jerome stands before an incomplete cross as Mary Magdalene sits on an unadorned throne. Jacob and his brother Esau exchange birthrights for lentils beside the risen Christ, His haunting red eyes, red hair, red face and blood contrasting against the pallor of His face. The apostles are caught in a storm in the Sea of Galilee beside the prophet David and Lazarus, resurrected.

I realize, of course, that my Spanish is insufficient to describe any of this.

The Señora suddenly stops talking, and looks over at me. "You look for an apartment here in Manta, just like your father?" she says, adding, half-mockingly: "I don't believe you."

"I would prefer to rent one in this building. You do have apartments for rent—"

"I don't understand. You have no wife? No children?"

"I do."

The Señora looks around, as though they might be lurking around a corner or beneath a window, awaiting a signal to enter.

"Then where are they?" she asks. "Why are you here, and they are in *Canadá*? Why did you leave them, just like your father left to you and your mother?"

I am silent.

"How you pay?" Yolanda asks abruptly in English. I reply that I have brought enough money for whatever payment was necessary.

They converse amongst themselves, and minutes later, after I pay for a month's rent and agree to teach the girls English in exchange for meals once or twice a day, I am thanking the Señora and her beautiful daughters and departing with a key.

5

THERE ARE TWO BEDROOMS in this dusty apartment, and a long windowed hallway that stretches out to provide an extended view of the beach. Three walls of the main living area are mostly comprised of windows.

An elongated balcony overlooks the inlet with a view of several fishing boats lying on their sides at low tide, one boat standing upright on stilts in the dehydrated bay. At the end of the hallway there is a sizeable washroom with a standing shower, which I soon discover produces more of a trickle than a shower.

My first dream in this new apartment is lucid and confused. I have been transformed into another person. I realize who I am, and I understand that I am dreaming, as happens in a lucid dream. There is the feeling, however, at least in my own mind, that I am someone else to those observing me. I have not been transformed into Kafka's monstrous vermin—nothing like that—but instead, I am a man who is prideful in believing himself to have transcended his former life, and to be somehow more adept at dealing with pain than those around him. A man, whose shadowy figure does not allow me to discern his identity, asks if I believe that as a result of my travels, I have somehow moved past the anger and guilt I have over my daughter—as though she has died.

"Yes," I reply definitively and too quickly, "I have."

"Gauguin," I continue a moment later, as though to further convince this stranger, who seems to doubt my words, "has done this, too. His pain was civilized society. Tahiti was his destination though, Paris his origin. Gauguin wanted a simpler life."

"Is that what you want, the abstraction of ostensible simplicity?" the stranger asks.

When I do not reply, he continues. *"Gauguin wanted to further his ambitions as a painter, but you are no painter."*

"Perhaps I could be."

"No. You have forsaken your wife and daughter and your chosen profession. How dare you compare your artwork to Gauguin's."

"I wasn't. You're misunderstanding. I could never—"

"Why are you here?"

"To see my father one last time."

"We both know that's not true. How could you possibly care about a man you only saw a few times, decades ago and knew only perfunctorily? And why are you staying?"

"I wanted to escape an existence where all that was pleasurable for me was found in the world of dreams, where waking thoughts were abhorrent and fear and panic would have consumed me. I wanted to embrace waking life instead of despising it—"

"You are disgraceful, shameful, and egotistical; your phrases are vapid and recited far too often in your thoughts. Panic and guilt still consume you. You of all people should recognize this. You still focus too much on dreams, just as you do on booze, even though you profess a desire to escape from a need for them. You are a dreamer and a drinker. You lack morals. You have abandoned everything and everyone, not only your wife and daughter but everyone you have ever known and cared for. You have left them behind, and for what? All for this dusty old apartment and such taunting dreams as this? You must see yourself as you truly are by attempting to comprehend yourself as any other incompetent clinical psychologist might ... Indeed, you have disgraced art by your comparison, you have disgraced your profession by deeming yourself competent, and you have left your country, your family and friends, along with your former life that you claim to have transcended. You made the decision that killed your daughter...."

"She's not dead."

"Not yet."

There is silence. The face behind the voice produces itself with the sudden appearance of daylight, but when I awaken to a knock on the door, its identity is immediately forgotten.

I am sweating beneath the thin sheet covering me. My eyes focus first on the fine mosquito netting around the bed. I jot down a few points, which I can later elucidate, in my dream journal. As my eyes adjust to the morning light, I look beyond the netting, out through the window and into the sea. There is another knock on the door. Startled, I stumble through the flaps of the netting and find myself standing abruptly upright.

I walk to the door. The metal scrapes along the floor as I open it to reveal a young woman, slender and striking and wearing a worn flowered skirt and a faded brown top, her golden hair tied back to fully expose the chiseled features of her face. Her face, her fingers and her frame are gaunt, and she has a slight belly which protrudes from beneath her shirt. She has an attractive elegance about her, in spite of her somewhat tattered appearance. She is holding a large collection of paints and several brushes, along with my privacy sign.

"*Hola,*" she says in a melodic tone, adding in English: "I came to invite you to a party."

She extends her hands toward me, offering me the paints and brushes, which I accept. "I found them on your doorstep." Handing me the sign, she adds: "And I found this on your doorknob. Really, you needn't bother with that. It's often difficult to sleep around here, no matter what you do."

"These painting supplies must be from the Señora," I say, aware that I am smiling now.

"She does love to paint," the woman says, also smiling. "So I've heard you're Canadian. I'm from Winnipeg myself. And you're from—"

"Toronto."

"Oh. Are you a painter?" She looks behind me inquisitively, as if expecting to find a room full of sketches and paintings.

"No," I say, shaking my head.

She looks disappointed. "So, you've come here for your father's funeral," she says. "I was sorry to hear that he died. He was sick for a long time...." She sighs, pauses for a breath, and then adds: "And you're staying here for a while, from what I understand, and under quite mysterious circumstances. No one seems to know why. You have no job, no ..." She stops. "But that's okay. We'll get to the bottom of that at my party.

I'm Karen, incidentally. I live directly above you. The party is at my apartment this Friday, if you're interested."

"I guess I won't be able to sleep then," I say, attempting to smile again, "so I'll have no choice in the matter."

6

I HAVE OFTEN MARVELED at the richness of dreams and the poverty of life. In my dreams, lavish adornments of the mind can perceive conversations with those both living and deceased, and grant the capability to move through time to see either the initiation or the termination of the world. Those manifestations are unsullied except to be subjected to the unfortunate whims and illogic of your own subconscious mind, and are inescapably tainted by the mundane and sometimes tragic realities of human existence. While we are wonderfully able to recall Freud's childhood "amnesia" in this dream world, to see the spinning of a cognitive web of our adult experiences and current knowledge suffused with these repressed childhood memories, we are invariably brought back into the cold light of practicality with each morning sun and with a few wretched pronouncements, such as the one made by my mother over the phone declaring that my father—with whom she would not let me live for a time as a child, saying that he cared for neither one of us—had died.

As a clinical psychologist utilizing techniques of dream analysis, the concept of dreams as an escape from such realities, and eventually contending with these truths through dream interpretation, has always interested me. I have studied, in detail, Freud's Austrian lectures—his relationship between manifest dreams (what is remembered) and latent (what is derived from the manifest dream after 'free association' analysis—what does this mean to you, quickly now, tell me, Freud might have said, using his understanding of substitution, allusion, imagery and symbolism to produce a dream meaning, the early Freud often interpreting a sexual one). I have learned the complicated theories of Jung, who was also interested in what the dream symbols mean to the dreamer in waking life. I understand Faraday's three levels of dream analysis—looking outward for direct meaning, looking at the dreamer's relation to symbols and settings, and looking inward by letting the symbols and settings speak for themselves. I also continuously study more contemporary viewpoints on the nature of dreams, but my attention always falls back to these three originators of dream analysis. And now, any attempt at escape from my reality through dreams is futile as I, along with the Señora, Inés and Yolanda, carry my father, who is wrapped in a shroud, and set him into the freshly-dug ground. We are all dressed in black, myself sweating in a black suede shirt and cotton pants, the Señora and her daughters in thin dresses that the Señora says she made herself. A few others, who are strangers to me, are lingering about.

Looking down as flowers, then his bagpipes, and then dirt are cast over top of him, I find myself wanting to dig with my hands in the dirt to unravel the shroud so I can see his face for one final time, as if to confirm that it was indeed he who had died and that this event was not some heartless ruse initiated by my mother and perpetuated by the Señora and her daughters to keep me from thinking and talking about my father, who is, in fact, still alive and living in a different part of Ecuador—Salinas or Quito or Guayaquil—while another gringo with the same slim build and musculature and skin tone, barely visible through the shroud, is buried in his place. I regret my earlier foolishness in leaving him covered from head to toe as we all ate rice with chicken and *ceviche* around him.

Despite the heartless and hypocritical ruse my father had perpetuated on me—promoting himself as a loving, caring father for the few times I was with him, and not the neglectful, abandoning, selfish man my mother and I knew him to be—I found that I could not help but love him. And seeing the dirt and the bagpipes and the flowers on top of him and the song of a chorus of birds in a nearby tree, the salt air and the cumulus clouds rolling over the ocean below us, I could also not help but feel a sense of awe and wonderment at what my father must have felt while standing here, over what would become his grave, in what the Señora pronounces as we walk away was his most beloved location in Manta, the place in which, with the view of the beach below, the prodigious backdrop of azure in the endless ocean and the infinite sky, he would play his bagpipes for hours with a few *cervezas* and a group of men who would gather here alongside him whenever they heard the air become laden with the heavy-set song of the sheepskin's wailing, the song echoing and drowning out any and all birdsong and bequeathing the vastness of this space with what must have been, on the best of days, his closest earthly approximation to the splendor of heaven.

As we walk down the hill and past the marina and over to the apartments in silence, I cannot stop thinking that the abandonment he perpetuated on my mother and me was at least briefly eradicated from his memory in such moments when, just as when my father and I would spend countless hours at the parties on the beach, nothing else seemed to matter....

7

THERE IS A CERTAIN unmistakable beauty in this land. This is a land transfixed on family, close friendships, and living life as though tomorrow's day might be the last. It is a land where it is easy to forget, where mothers kiss the bellies of babies they hold high above their heads, beside concrete homes with the glow of a single light bulb emanating from within; where, on this evening, the smooth melody of guitar and voice permeates the smooth hushing of the sea to the shore and the crackling of firewood. It is a land where an improvised dance floor has been created in the sand, where the shoes of young and old have been cast aside, where the smells of salt, lime, liquor, body sweat, and burning palm leaves infuse the air with an aura free from anxiety, free from tension and fear, and free from the worries of living.

I awaken to see a crowd dissipating in the hallway outside Karen's apartment, and I follow the party down to the beach. The flames of the fire seem to dance in rhythm with the music, just as the sea seems to. I sit down on the cold sand as Karen approaches me, her slim body outlined by her meagre dress and the light of the fire. In this light, she looks astonishingly like Yelena.

"You are late," she says. "You missed most of the party."

"I was dreaming," I say placidly.

I do not tell her that I was dreaming again of Yelena, standing in a closet, or that I had written an alternate ending to the dream on paper before falling asleep, in order to put an end to it. *"What are you doing here?"* I asked Yelena in the dream. *"You know,"* Yelena's voice replied. But the sounds of conversation awakened me, and the dream terminated too early. I had awoken to the sound of people in Karen's hallway upstairs.

"It has been said before," I say, "that the body can do better without sleep—"

"—than the mind can do without dreams. I've heard that too. So, you were dreaming. Trying to shed what your waking mind can't accept. What's so bad about this place that you can't endure? I'm surprised you could even sleep, let alone dream, with a party going on above your head. You must be a very sound sleeper."

"Most of the time, yes."

Karen sits down beside me. For a moment, we both watch the dancers moving to the music's rhythm. The dancing stops as the guitar is passed to a man with long hair grown past his waist, who immediately begins playing.

"I've seen it at every party I've been to since I've lived here," Karen says. "The ritual passing of the guitar. I can't play, but it doesn't matter because they never pass the guitar to women anyway … here, take a drink."

She hands me a small glass flask.

"I don't drink."

"Everyone drinks."

"I don't. It causes problems for me."

There is silence. She continues watching the dancers as she shifts her weight in the sand. She lights a cigarette.

"Have you been here long?" I ask.

"Two years," she says, exhaling. "It's a long time for me to have stayed in one place. And what about you? How long are you going to be here?"

"I don't know," I reply. "A month, maybe longer."

"Are you a teacher?" she asks. "Are you looking for work?"

"I'm a psychologist. And I'm not looking for work, particularly."

"A psychologist? What do you do for money, here?" She pauses and then, after a moment, acquiescing to my silence, adds: "If I can ask, of course."

"I've brought enough, but I'm going to be teaching English to Inés and Yolanda," I say. "In exchange for one or two meals a day."

"How resourceful of you. The Señora is a very good cook. She's asked me to tutor her daughters in the past, and I did, months ago, but not since. I've taught enough English to last a lifetime." She draws from her cigarette, pauses, and then continues.

"They both want to go to New York, the sisters. The Señora doesn't want to move, even though her husband and her daughters' father is there. He works in construction in Brooklyn. Have they told you that?"

"No."

"They will."

She pauses for a while as we listen to the music, and we watch as a pair of dancers falls down in the sand, laughing. "I had a man," she continues, "a friend of the sisters, offer to marry me."

"Really?"

"Yes. Don't sound so surprised. All of my students want to go to either Miami or New York. It's not easy to get there if you were born here. If they have relatives living in the US, which Inés and Yolanda do, then they can get a visa. But it takes time; years, sometimes a decade or even more. But as I was saying, the man who offered to marry me, I dated him for a while and I explained to him that I lived in Winnipeg, not in Miami or New York, but he didn't seem to care or to even know the difference. To him it was all the same. I told him I wasn't planning to go back to Winnipeg anyway, and I talked him into going to school instead of marrying me. So he moved to an island off the coast of Venezuela, where his family is from, and he is studying business at a technical university there. Even though he writes to me often, I almost never reply...." She pauses, and then rubs her forehead. "Sorry, I'm rambling. I've had too much to drink."

Karen raises the cigarette to her lips. A woman in a skirt falls while dancing, and is promptly collected and returned to an upright position by the throng of dancers. There is almost no disruption of the flow of movement, as if she was a piece of debris unfettered and swept along by the current at the bottom of the sea.

"You know," Karen continues, "I teach down at the university. I can get you a job there. It wouldn't be a problem.

Really. I'm the only native English-speaking teacher there, and I may not be there for long."

"Why, where are you going?"

"Let's not talk of that tonight," she says, extinguishing her cigarette in the sand. Then, taking my hand, she leads me into the mass of dancers.

8

THE SEÑORA HAS LEFT my father's possessions, which she promised me, on the kitchen table in my apartment. After making a cup of instant coffee, I sit down in the early morning and sort through them. I find they are comprised of a few photographs of him hiking through the jungle, a handwritten letter of sale for a group of huts there, and a collection of clothing and other miscellaneous items, all from the vacant apartment next to Karen's upstairs. There is also a letter from Yelena here, and I sit down at the table and tear the envelope apart, reading through parts of it quickly.

Even though I don't know why you've left—other than you need no one but yourself, and maybe you're out to prove it—here's something to keep you company. I've been doing a story for the library newsletter about Malcolm Forsyth. He won Canadian Composer of the year back in '89. He is from South Africa and brings diversity to Canada. I listened to an interview with him on the radio. He is the embodiment of what makes Canada so rich. Everyone brings a piece of their past with them, a part of their culture, and of course their own reminiscences. This is what you brought with you when you went away to Ecuador. You'll never lose your memory or your experience. No matter how much you try to forget, or to run, you can never be far enough away to escape your own mind....

A while later I settle back into bed, my body still exhausted from the evening before but my mind alert from the effects of the coffee, and I eventually fall asleep after reading the letter over and over again. I fall into dreams of singing and dancing Zulus, half naked with dark skin, their arms immobile at their sides as they dance, shields in their hands shaped to appear as if they are the overgrown leaves of the giant baobab trees, and covered with decorative fur and leopard skin. Their staves and torches and heads are held high in the air in front of fires and beehive huts, these men somehow becoming ingrained into the pages of orchestral compositions—D-flat major for trumpets and horns, and E major for violas and basses. They sit on the pages like dormant spirits waiting to be played into life.

Theirs is a smooth transition from the pages, once they're brought forth, through the conduit of the overture and my father's bagpipes, into the ears of the listeners—shifting melodies of Canadian, Scottish and African harmonization....

9

IN THE FEW TIMES that I see Karen in the weeks that follow, in between receiving a few letters from Yelena, I discover some details about Karen's past. She has not been back to Winnipeg in almost twelve years. She has been traveling from country to country, securing work mainly teaching English, sweeping floors, and waitressing. She worked on a Kibbutz in Israel and picked grapes in Greece, earning enough to travel from Spain to Portugal, through France and over to England and north to Norway. She ended her European tour in St. Petersburg, Russia but she couldn't find work there as she spoke very little Russian, and all the jobs seemed to require fluency. She dated a man in the Russian military who left in order to engage in training exercises on the sea of Japan for what she said was far too long, and as he was travelling the sixteen days it took to get back across northern Mongolia, through parts of Kazakhstan and Siberia and back to St. Petersburg, she was making the necessary arrangements to return to a place where she once lived and worked—Ecuador.

"I've told you everything about myself," Karen says to me one afternoon as we are sitting in plastic chairs on a bar patio, drinking Pilsners beside a busy street. "So, tell me: what leads you to stay in this country? And in Manta, of all places? Are you running away from something? Someone?"

Even though she professes to have apprised me of all of the details of her life, I sense that she has only intimated at them and is deliberately withholding the sentiments and motivations I demand of both patients and friends. At the same time, I have a desire to share her same experiences; not only to know more about them, but to know for myself the places to which she has travelled. I don't feel as though I want to disclose any of this to her now, though, and so I try to think of an obscure answer which she might be able to correlate to her own situation.

"I'm running toward something," I reply, unsure of how I might continue this.

"What's that?" she asks.

I pause. I have begun her line of questioning, and I comprehend that because of Karen's constant travelling, she has a frequent need to understand, and to be understood, by strangers. I suddenly experience a tinge of this same urge myself.

"I took Thoreau's advice," I say, incredulous at my own words, "to live the life I've always imagined."

"And this is it, living here in Manta? Really? The life you've always imagined?"

"It is," I reply emphatically, sitting up in my chair.

"You're crazy," she says, smiling.

"So how well did you know my father?" I ask.

She pauses and takes a deep breath just before a taxi kicks up dust and billows exhaust fumes beside us. She coughs before answering.

"I knew him a little, saw him around at parties. He taught English at the university whenever he needed money. He kept to himself most of the time. The Señora talked as though she loved him. They went out together one night, and she said it was the most enjoyable night of her life. They went from bar to bar, *discoteca* to *discoteca*, and he played the bagpipes as she entered each place. He 'piped her in', as she put it. And when she asked him when they were going to get married, your father simply said that she was too young for him, when they both knew she was actually twenty years older and separated from, but still legally married to a man who lived thousands of miles away in New York, while he was still legally married to your mother." She pauses to take a drink.

"So, are you married?" she asks.

I touch the ring in my pocket.

"Yes," I reply, to which she appears surprised.

"Children?"

"Sort of."

I hand her a copy of the ultrasound picture, and she scoffs.

"Oh."

"My wife is much older than I am. The baby has Down syndrome, and it isn't developing properly. The doctor says the fetus has clubbed feet and a head that is too small for her body, and she'll have heart defects and mental problems. I'm giving my wife time, and writing her letters, to prevent her from making the worst mistake of her life. She wants to have her pregnancy terminated."

Karen doesn't ask me any more questions and, as we sit there in silence, quickly finishing our beers before leaving, I suddenly realize that I have never said those words to anyone else.

10

Although months seem to have passed since I've been here, it has only been weeks. I am able to understand the Señora and her daughters now from my limited Spanish, providing they speak clearly and not too fast. I am at the stage of language learning where I'm too busy mentally dissecting verbs and categorizing social interactions into statements or questions, to engage in a true conversation. Inés and Yolanda have learned enough from my lessons to have simple conversations in English, and the Señora seems pleased with their progress.

I first touched brush to what passes for canvas here a week ago. The oil colours mix on the page before me at noon to form the outline of a boat, the stilts beneath it gleaming in the sun. That was a difficult effect to achieve, and I have a dozen ruined pages to prove it. The colours blend on the page to produce the background which surrounds fishing boats in the distance, a man splashing in the water nearby beside umbrellas and lemonade vendors. The clouds are simply brushstrokes, dotted first and then rotated. In my dreams these brushstrokes, even before I produced them on paper, turned from dragons to butterflies to the portrait of an elderly man, my father, holding onto his bagpipes, with his kilt and all of his associated accoutrements.

I put my paintbrush down and examine a letter Yelena has just sent:

You know that Van Gogh was once a preacher? His first sermon, it was said, could only have been written by an artist. It was too descriptive for anyone else. He lived with evangelicals, sleeping on straw mats and wearing rags. His only reflection later, about being a preacher, was that he missed shapes and pictures. You might say he was insane. Everyone believed that his mind had gone, and not without reason. Others say he was just epileptic.

He lived on absinthe, bread and coffee, and he also consumed paint as he licked his brush so frequently. He lived in constant malnutrition and poverty and was institutionalized not because he tried to swallow his paints as a form of suicide, and not because he wore a hat full of candles when he painted at night, but because of an incident with Gauguin. He knew Gauguin, and might have lived with him in Paris. The incident involved a brothel, Gauguin, and a severed ear. You can say that Van Gogh was an insane man among the sane, or maybe you would say the reverse. His last painting went for eighty-four million dollars—

I begin another painting, one of Annabelle, after setting up her ultrasound picture on the edge of the desk. I add swirls and flecks of grey skin to the page and, growing suddenly tired, I close my door and fall through the mosquito netting, now shimmering in the midday sun, and into my lumpy bed, away from the absurdity of the world that is now awake outside, and into the world of dreams....

11

FREUD SPEAKS: *"In dream censorship, the unconscious mind struggles to express those desires which are too difficult for the waking mind to accept ... they are encoded messages, knowing they are subject to interpretation by the waking mind. You, and only you, will determine their true meaning when you are conscious. But only if you so desire ... and beware of what you might find...."*

Jung retorts: *"How do you explain that, as per my contention, we continually dream even when awake, and according to your belief, distressing thoughts are subdued and overpowered by the unconscious mind? We are receiving encoded messages, then, all the time? How do you explain reality? Is our unconscious mind constantly struggling to suppress anything which is difficult to accept, even in real life? Is our own supposed reality, then, just what we want to see, and nothing more?"*

I interject: *"I'm trying to sleep, and here you are filling my head with nonsense. Jung, you're assuming both contentions to be true, and making a deduction from that. You can't—"*

Plato, inexplicably, utilizing his own exact words: *"The good are those who content themselves with dreaming of what others, the wicked, actually do."*

I begin again: *"You're saying, Freud, that the unconscious mind disguises things too painful for the conscious mind to experience. You, Jung, are saying that even our reality can be nothing other than what we want to see, because we're constantly dreaming—if we accept both your premises, that is. And Plato, you are saying that something too painful for us to experience is not as painful for the wicked, if they have a suppressed and distorted view of reality or not...."*

They shake their heads. *No, no, no. You are no philosopher, and not much of a psychologist. You are no painter, either.*

Kerouac, inexplicably: *"Unrequited love. It's such a bore...."*

12

I AM SITTING IN the Señora's apartment, consuming rice and beans with Ecuadorian soft cheese and orange juice. Her daughters are busy cleaning some dishes, and I ask if they've already eaten.

"They have," the Señora says in a hushed Spanish. She is sitting in a chair close to mine. She looks over at her daughters, and raises her voice: "Inés, go to Karen's apartment. Bring her back here. You invite her here, to eat with us."

Inés immediately drops the towel she's using to dry the dishes, and slips quietly through the heavy front door. This rouses the dog at the back of the house, who barks as if to show he is still on guard. The Señora yells something at the dog in a Spanish I don't understand.

As Yolanda places a plate of steaming food in front of the empty chair beside me, her fragrance of a floral vanilla briefly overpowering the scent of the food, the Señora asks me if I'm dating Karen. I say that I am not.

"I wonder at times about Karen," she says, eyeing the painted figures around her. "Why does she travel so much? Why does she never see her home? Do you wonder this, too?"

"I don't know," I say, shrugging my shoulders as I eat.

The Señora looks confused.

When I am nearly finished my lunch, Inés returns with Karen, who finds a seat beside me. Inés returns to her duties and the dog begins barking again.

"Eat," the Señora says, rising from her seat to address Karen, and indicating the plate of hot food in front of her. "Rice and beans with cheese."

Karen greets everyone in the room with a nod of her head, thanks the Señora, and begins eating.

The Señora reclaims her seat while maintaining her focus on Karen. "Why do you never see your home and your mother?" she asks.

"I don't know," Karen says.

"That is what Jonathan told me also," the Señora says. "He, too, does not know why."

"You were all just talking about me?"

I work quickly to finish my lunch, and then I rise to leave.

"Sit down," Karen says, pulling me back into my seat. Looking at me, she adds: "Did you start all this?"

"I was wondering," the Señora continues, glancing over at Karen, "if you miss your home."

Karen continues eating, and Inés places a glass of juice in front of her. Karen picks up the glass, takes a drink and gazes at the Señora.

"There's nothing for me there," Karen says. "That's all. It's just too sad to think about—my childhood of physical and mental abuse, my parents who fought all the time—so really, I don't. But despite all that, yes, I still miss it, just as I think anyone misses their home when they move away from it. Even so, I'll never go back."

Everyone is silent. The dishes clang together as they are placed in cupboards with no doors. The dog barks one last time, and then becomes quiet.

Karen waits for a moment, and finishes her juice before continuing: "You should ask Jonathan that same question. He has a wife and baby on the way back home."

"He is not here for long," the Señora says. "But you are."

"I have a feeling he will be here longer than I will," Karen says, looking at me before turning her attention back to her plate. "Just a feeling."

The Señora directs her attention toward me now. She asks about my family.

"I have a wife, who is a librarian at a local university, and we have a child on the way," I reply, without offering to show the only picture I brought of Yelena, or the ultrasound, certain that the Señora would not know what an ultrasound is, and certain that she would not understand what Yelena has contemplated in talking about ending the baby's life due to its supposed imperfections. "My mother raised me, and I never knew my father very well, apart from my few visits here. My mother is rather conservative, albeit an alcoholic as a result of my father's departure, set in her job as a teacher and as a patron at a local tavern with no plans to retire from either. My father, as you probably know, idolized Kerouac and his lifestyle. I read all of Kerouac's books as a result, even his obscure, rambling diaries and poems that really should've been left in obscurity or in the realm of discarded thought. I read a book written by the South American Kerouac, Che Guevara, who travelled all around this continent with a friend on a motorcycle."

The Señora, confused, turns toward Karen, who translates all of what I have just said, which I now realize was communicated in a mixture of English and bad Spanish, into the Señora's native tongue.

"Ah, ya," the Señora says, continuing to speak, this time in a rapid Spanish interspersed with local expressions, none of which I can understand.

When she finally finishes, I ask Karen: "What did she say?"

"She says your father used to play the bagpipes on the spot overlooking the ocean, where he was buried, all the time, whenever he wanted to forget. She said they must have been able to hear him all the way over in China. And she said that he, like you, ran away from his family. She says, not in so many words, that something tormented him about being here, away from his family, and she sees that same anguish and suffering in you. She thinks it was his family back in Canada, you and your mother, that made him resentful when she half-jokingly talked of marriage with him. It was as though the word marriage, when repeated, infused him with a tremendous guilt, just as, whenever he saw a child on the street, it must have reminded him of you … she says he had a touch of hubris, which is why he never went back, and why he died here."

"Hubris?"

"Well, she said it as *arrogancia*. Arrogance, excessive pride, it's all the same. After he left you and your mother, his ego would never let him reverse his decision, which became somehow more resolute over time, and so the years and the decades simply passed with him here, and you and your mother there. Quite sad, actually."

As I listen only peripherally for the sound of my name while they continue their conversation, the meaning of my recurring dream of a closed closet door, with the sense that Yelena is inside, suddenly becomes somewhat more clear when I combine the Señora's statement with one of Jung's contentions. Jung asserted—when discussing the mother and the womb, the body and the physiological, that which creates and symbolizes the fundamentals of consciousness—that confinement suggests the nocturnal and a condition of nervous apprehension.

The panic and anxiety I experience at night, sometimes with that dream and sometimes without, might be ended through reaching out in my dream to expand beyond the simple confines of the one closet door, where I might encounter my mother in the darkness, and another closet door, beyond which I would sense my father, who I am told always fought bitterly with my mother whenever they were together, perhaps staring at an endless series of closet doors with my same sense of remorse and shame, undertaking no actions to reconcile with the source of his sorrow, apart from the unwitting sensation of having experienced such sentiments.

∞

"You know, the Señora's daughters have applied for a visa to go to New York to be with their father," Karen says to me later, as we step away from the apartment and walk barefoot toward the beach. "The Señora applied for one too, but I can't see her ever going there. It's obvious to me that she has never left Manta. At least, never for long."

"Maybe she's trying to understand what might happen if she does," I say.

13

I WRITE A LETTER asking Yelena to come here, not simply to visit after Annabelle is born, as I wrote in the previous letter, but now, to live. Here, Annabelle would not be judged, I write, but accepted. Her life would be better here. After living here for a time, we would all travel the earth together, working as much as we needed to in order to obtain money for further travel.

Over the next few days, I think of freedom and the myriad of possibilities before me. I imagine that I can see all of the immensity of life through the anticipation of travel along with Yelena and Annabelle, and through the windows of this apartment and the ocean it overlooks.

I have the intuition as I mail the letter that all of the burdens of my previous existence have been lifted and that emancipation has been granted to me through this place.

I no longer need to go anywhere in the mornings. I paint endlessly. I don't teach the Señora's daughters until late in the afternoon, after they have returned home from the university. The Señora tells me that they do not have to pay to attend the university, only for books, and that they do not have to pay for my tutoring services except by tolerating my presence in their house, which she says is no payment at all.

∞

This evening is unique in my own personal history. I have only experienced insomnia infrequently, with increased stress, and I have never simply wandered about aimlessly at night. Despite my recently apparent euphoria, I cannot sleep. Wondering what Yelena is doing at this moment, thinking she would be reading late into the night with her endless cups of tea, I am relegated to roaming the streets, feeling as though I am in a lucid dream—the beaches, the stores and businesses are caged with retracting metal guards for the night, and the strange-looking women and tired-looking men seem too distracted by whatever it is they are looking for to notice me roving about. It is a strange world, that of the insomniac. It is a different view of humanity here, not one I would ever imagine myself proud to be a part of. It is a world that evolves after the curtains have been closed along the streets, long after the families have fallen into sleep. The families are secure with the broken bottle shards extending over their concrete fences, and with the guard dogs on their roofs. They are protected by these defenses against unwanted entry. They are sheltered in their fortifications against an immoral land of drug users and pushers, sexual gluttony and lust, and alcohol and tobacco. They are locked away against this land of excess and against this unseen city, which has now been unveiled before my eyes.

There is the sound of music in the distance. As I walk toward it, a familiar figure appears from between dozens of abandoned buckets and elongated poles belonging to shrimp fishermen. I recognize the shape as Karen. She is dressed entirely in black. Her hair is pinned back. She is very attractive in this light.

"Jonathan," she says, hugging me. She dangles a lit cigarette in one hand and a large glass smelling like sweetened turpentine, likely *Caña Manabita* sugarcane alcohol, in the other. She releases me after a moment.

"*Venga*," she says, walking away and extending her hand for me to follow. "Come here. Come and have a drink with me."

"This explains why I never see you during the day," I say.

"This doesn't explain anything. We're having a drink, that's all."

"I don't drink."

"No explanations."

I grasp her hand as she lifts the glass to my lips to give me a long drink. She leads me somberly into a small group of people, all of them engaged in conversations in the rapid-speak and localized expressions of Ecuadorian coastal Spanish.

They all extend their hands toward mine, in the proper sequence according to Karen's introductions. Afterward she hands me her drink again, and as I down some more she tells me that they are mostly students and some professors.

"I thought you weren't going to explain anything," I say.

"Well, that was the only one tonight," she replies. "Apart from this: if you weren't married, if I wasn't—involved—I might be tempted to kiss you right now. Softly, on the lips." She smiles.

There is a fire beside us, a spitting grill sputtering the venom of fishy lime juice. There is a much larger fire nearby, students and faculty dancing barefoot around it, eating the flesh of freshly caught fish beneath the moonlight as if in some pagan ritual. There are several beautiful women standing beside the fire from whom I can't seem to turn my attention away. Inés and Yolanda are among these women, and the sisters smile in my direction. Karen notices my distraction and, turning my head toward her, she hands me her drink. Feeling the effects now, I take another mouthful.

"I'm flying out of Guayaquil," she announces as she casts her shoes away. "In two days."

"Where are you going?"

"Well if you must know, and I assume you must because you asked: Caracas, Venezuela. There's a small island off the coast. My friend who goes to school there, I'm going to see him."

"Why?"

She pauses, and then sighs. "Well, I haven't told you, and I don't want you to tell the Señora. When I'm ready to, I'll tell her myself."

"Tell her what?"

"More explanations," she says, sighing again. "Tell her that I'm pregnant."

I am silent for a moment, thinking of her smoking, her drunkenness, wondering about possible damage to the fetus, and I immediately think of harm coming to my own daughter. I have the impulsive urge, thinking of this, to go home, to protect my daughter from those who would do her harm. I have not received any letters from Yelena recently, although I have been writing to her now more than ever before, trying to entice her to come here. I could only know her state of mind through those letters, in which she wrote nothing about our child, and now I have no recourse to know anything about either of them.

I return to the conversation, reflecting that I've never seen Karen with a man.

"You're pregnant by whom?" I ask.

"The man I'm going to see in Venezuela," she replies.

"Oh. So you won't be back?"

"I can't give up on that apartment. One day soon, I'll be back."

I pause for a moment before stating emphatically, while thinking of my daughter again: "I'm going with you."

"To Venezuela?" she asks incredulously.

"No. To the airport."

"So am I. But where are you going?"

"I'm going home. To Canada."

"Really? Interesting ..."

Among the students and professors, we move in rhythm to the *salsa* and *merengue* music in a ritual dance to our trip, to our safety, to a glamorous freedom I have never known. I have never known insomnia to be anything but terrifying, but now it is sensuality, uninhibited. Now it is spirituality. It is a faded opera soprano that comes from the sea. It is the voice of Annabelle, soft and sweet, fluttering like the wind through the leaves of the palm trees. It is anything but logical, this feeling.

Seven years of abundance, seven years of drought for you Pharaoh, God said in His infinite wisdom.

Dreams, one of God's instruments for speaking to the individual. Did He intend for psychologists to interpret dreams?

Prophets, God's Dream interpreters, recipients of a divine word helping form the basis of faith.

Jacob's ladder, extending to heaven.

God, the Compassionate, the Merciful.

The Warrior. The Father. The Creator. The Destroyer.
Without dream images, would there be any religion?
Without God, life is meaningless.
Without my dreams, without my visions by day and night, what
would I have?

14

THE NEXT MORNING, I awaken with the memory of what was certainly one of the worst nocturnal panic attacks I've ever experienced. Sunlight beams through the windows and I am tired, thinking that, instead of contemplating what I endured the night before, desperately attempting to forget my dread as my heart pounded rhythmically to the pulse of the waves lapping onto the beach, I must focus on other thoughts.

I contemplate how to make "legitimate" art.... First, choose a worthy subject: Karen ... not falling, or sweating, but standing upright, unaffected by any form of physical exertion ... choose an incomprehensible message: that her dreams are like chilled wine, dry or sweet, white or red, rich in tannins, intense and spicy, complex in flavour ... her dreams do not fill her with terror without the accompanying nightmares ... try to forget ... choose a background: her departure ... the time has come to make "legitimate" art.

I sketch her as she sleeps for the first time, at her request made the previous evening, in my apartment, on my couch. It is mid-morning. From her spasmodic movements I am aware that she is dreaming some awful dream, which she may not remember upon awakening—unless, of course she awakens quickly and has time to recall the events before her conscious mind suppresses and overpowers her unconscious thoughts ... she shifts one way, then another ... then suddenly, she opens her eyes. She tells me she remembers a bus ... there were cliffs, too ... the university above, the sky below ... the bus fell over the cliff's edge, and into the red sky. She was falling, endlessly falling....

I work to somehow capture the essence of fright in her face. This is a way to remember, I say as she watches me. I am sketching a crude picture of her dream images now. This is a dream diary of sorts, I explain. A mnemonic trigger to recollect some of the events of the dream.

She dismisses her dream. It was ridiculous, she says. What colour was the bus? I ask her as I begin to paint. *Red*, she says, *the same as the students and the sky*. Were you on it? *I don't know. I think so*. What about the cliff, what shape was it? *More rounded than any cliff should be*. The university? *The same as it is in normal life*. You don't see the meaning, then? *No*. The one constant is your work, the students and the bus the same colour as the sky, the students all merging together into one memory, the rounded cliffs early Freud would say are your breasts and I would say it is your inability to attach yourself to any one person or place. Falling in dreams has to do with a lack of control. The myth that you will die in your sleep if you hit the bottom is just that, a myth. I've had many patients who have hit the bottom and still, they have woken up. Still, I hope I never hit the bottom.

As I paint, I recall how I have recently dreamed of falling. Sometimes Annabelle is there falling along with me, her tiny body wrapped in the same cloth as my father's shroud. We have never met earth. The land below is always black, the same as the darkness that surrounds us, but somehow I know it is there. Despite my knowledge that my death would not come as I hit it, the subliminal realization that it was there always prompted me into consciousness.

Are you psychoanalyzing me? Karen asks.

Perhaps, I say, adding after a moment: well, actually, yes. A while later, with a look of patent disgust on her face as her eyes move from what she says to be one disturbing image to another, from the picture of her dream to other pencil sketches and paintings scattered about, she suddenly and resolutely declares: *You are no artist. No artist at all.*

15

THERE ARE TIMES WHEN I am convinced that I see someone from Canada who I know, walking on the streets of Manta, and I realize afterward that all those around me must be strangers. The notion of their assumed identity defies my sense of logic. Still, I have seen past patients and family members in the crowds, and friends from my childhood walking on the streets alone or staring back at me from a corner bar.

This is one of those moments when I believe I see someone I have thought about but have not seen in over a month. She is across the street, contemplating whether to purchase a sweatshirt, a *sudadera*. Something to keep warm in.

I think for a moment that perhaps I am mistaken, that this woman is Karen, until I look again.

I never expected to see her here. She never answered my letters asking her to come.

She looks the same, her hair drooping from her shoulders in flaxen, rolling waves, her body thin, and well-defined by the folds of her dress. Her face is refined with feline features—especially her eyes...those deep green, penetrating feline eyes...She has returned to allow me the opportunity to save Annabelle, before I have the chance to return to where I assumed they were.

Yelena! I shout. She looks around, and doesn't see me. I walk toward her, smiling, ecstatic.

I know that this exact scene will melt into my dreams. I know it may become lucid because I am thinking about having this dream later. We have the power to create a lucid dream by thinking dream thoughts during the day. By thinking I can fly to her, or reach out to her with an enormous hand, or contact her through mind-thought, I can later dream this exact scene and know I am dreaming—thereby having control over it. It will become a waking dream.

She is cold, she says as I approach her. She did not expect to be cold here. She puts the sweater on over her dress. It is nearly nighttime, I say. *I see the moon,* she says, *it's larger than other moons I've seen. And redder. Look, it's blood red. It's a hook moon. And it's sinking into the horizon. I've never seen that, either.*

I notice, for the first time, that she is cradling a small baby in her arms, a baby with the most beautiful face I've ever seen. *This is Annabelle,* she says. The baby's eyes are closed.

This is the first time I've seen you in over a month, I say. And you haven't written any letters lately.

Of course, you know where we've been, Yelena says. *You ran away from us, not the other way around. You see me here, in your new home, and think maybe that you never left. A piece of your home, a part of your past has come back for you. How does that make you feel? Are you distraught by our presence? Are you upset, or pleased? I can't tell by your expression. It could be either. I can see in your face that you are tired. You haven't been sleeping. Wasn't it you who told me how the mind cannot do well without dreams? Have you been dreaming, or have you been forsaking your dreams as you said you would?*

Oh, you are preposterous with your dreams, you know you are. There is so much to say ... I'm only here for a short time ... how to begin ... clichéd questions always end in clichéd answers ... Have you learned any Spanish since you've been gone? Have you been to the mountains, to the rainforest? You have? To the mountains, but not the rainforest. I see. We can go to the rainforest together. I know of a place where you get a guide to take you through ... I've heard about it before from other people who have been there ... we can see termite nests in the trees, swing from vine roots high above the forest floor ... we can trek by the trails and eat fish straight from the Amazon ... we can kayak and white water raft ... you've thought about this too, have you? You have seen this in your dreams? You're unforgivable, you know, leaving without even asking us to come with you. How could you not even ask? You and your silly dreams. You have an established career, your own practice, and who are your patients visiting now? Look at you. You're dishevelled; not disgustingly so, but almost. You've turned into Gauguin in Tahiti, or into Van Gogh as a preacher, but without their gifts. Are you malnourished? You can't be eating right, look at you. You're too thin. You're a beach dweller, a nomad. You ought to be ashamed of yourself. No, I'm sorry … I take that back. Maybe I should be ashamed of myself for saying that … but you've only been gone, what, a month, or a month and a half, and look at you. You should have some pride in yourself, if you're going to be chasing after Ecuadorian women. Have you met anyone here? Are you searching for someone? What is your purpose here? Why are you staying here in Manta, because your father lived here before? What was he doing here for so long? Was it a woman? Why did he come here initially? You said before that he never truly acknowledged having had a family, and his escape was through being here in this place and through alcoholism, an extended vacation, one that in his case lasted decades—but why Manta? Was it a manta ray he saw in a dream, like one of those fish that swim above the bottom of the sea, and then he found this place on a map and somehow connected the two? Was he as preposterous as you? Remember, you're the ridiculous one, not me. His wife, your mother, was she from here? No? He had little money, wanted to live a lifetime on it paying the Señora twenty or thirty dollars a month for rent and food, and found a school that needed English teachers in an obscure and isolated fishing village in an obscure and isolated part of the globe? I'm sorry, I'm rambling, I've been drinking a bit, I'm sorry if you don't think that's right in my condition, but did you really want to be here, away from all those you love? A place, after all, is only as good as the people who inhabit it. Why did you want to leave? Why do you stay away? How much longer will you remain? You said you would be away for a month, but you've already been gone that long and you haven't returned. You're going to, you say? Really? Or do you plan to stay here as long as your father did? Is this to become the ultimate egoistical endeavor of your life, your dreams amplified? Dreams are egoistic, you always liked to quote Freud. He said dreams were the ultimate form of egoism, did you know that? Of course, you must know that. You probably even told me that. I can't tell you anything you don't know about him. But listen, when were you truly planning on coming back to see us? And what are the demons that have chased you away? Your daughter, look she's opened her eyes, and she's looking at you now. She's telling you

*that she needs you, look, I'll unravel her tiny blanket so you can see
her clubbed feet. She's smelling you now. Babies are sensitive, even
to the smells of their father....*
Are you really coming home?

16

YELENA AND ANNABELLE ARE in my apartment. Not simply my visual impression of them but their voices, their bodies, their souls. This is the first time I've ever seen them sleeping together on my bed, making the same outline as Karen had as I painted her on the couch.

Yelena is solemn and sweet in her sleep. Annabelle is a symphony of silence.

Yelena has changed. She is an adventurer, and has followed me here. She has never been far from her homes in Canada and Russia before—except for when I finally convinced her to go to Spain with me. She lived in Russia until she was six, when her family moved to Canada. She described the Russian wheat fields in the region near Moscow where she lived, golden and flowing, with the wind beneath wide expanses of sky, that have produced themselves to me in my sleeping moments.

She is comfortable in her loneliness, she has told me before. What does this mean? Am I as comfortable in my own as I profess to be?

My paint brush flicks along the lines of Yelena's body from the nape of her neck to the small of her back, down to the extent of her polished toenails. After creating a single portrait of Yelena I go on to paint a multitude of different views of Annabelle. *She is exquisite, a baby Greek goddess. Look at those tiny, as yet unformed fingers. She is baby Aphrodite, singing amidst the foaming waves of the sea. She is born in, and will rise from, the sea.*

Annabelle stirs. The form is blurred, inconstant, changing. My brush moves with her, caresses her, forms her outline anew once again. Her form is the sincerity and the reliability of change.

Annabelle rises to sit vertically on the bed and rubs her eyes. She yawns, and stretches a baby feline stretch. Looking over at the sky outside, I see that it is overcast for the first time that I've been here. I have a difficult time accepting that Annabelle and Yelena, who is still sleeping, are here in front of me.

I imagine with fear that they are sadly strangers with similar features to those I have known, who upon closer inspection are revealed to be unfamiliar to me....

17

"HAVE YOU BEEN TO *the mountains, to the rainforest? You have?* *To the mountains, but not the rainforest. We can go together, I* *know of a place where you get a guide to take you through … we* *can see termite nests in the trees, swing from vine roots high above* *the forest floor … we can trek by the trails and eat fish straight* *from the Amazon … we can kayak and white water raft …you've* *thought about this, have you? You've seen this in your dreams?"*

I recall Yelena's words as I set out with Karen for the bus station. The man with the dusty taxicab, who welcomed me to Manta, inquires, with a grin, whether I'll be back.

"Wet season will soon be here," he says in Spanish, looking skyward. "Still, many places of this country remain flooded from El Niño."

"I will be back to see the wet season," I reply, boarding the bus with Karen. Yelena and Annabelle, sadly, are gone. My copy of Boccaccio's *Decameron*, which I hold beneath my arm, plunks with a cloud of dust onto the street. Quickly retrieving it, I place the worn volume in my backpack.

I will go to Peru some day, I say to Karen as we find our seats on the bus bound for Quito. I don't explain to her how my father never had such intense dreams as he had there. It was because of the thin mountain air, my father said, a lack of oxygen combined with what he called the spiritual energy of the place. He dreamed of oversized condors with supernatural energies laced with gemstones and jewels, of the beginning and the end of the world, the end coming with fire-breathing dragons flying over barren landscapes. He dreamed of angels allowing him access to a telephone which he could use to talk with anyone, living or dead, which he used to talk at length with a friend of his who had died in a motorcycle accident. I told my father something he didn't like because he said it was something my mother would say, and in fact my mother had taught me once that speaking to the dead is abhorrent to God and that the reason for King Saul's death was his consultation first with the witch of Endor and then with the spirit of Samuel.

Karen says nothing for a long time. I know what she is thinking. We've had the conversation only hours before. We couldn't go to Peru now, even if we had the time, as we wouldn't get past the Ecuadorian-Peruvian border. They're at war, those two countries. It's too dangerous to leave to go anywhere, the Señora told us, adding that we should stay very close to home and try not to leave our apartments for at least a week or two.

"The protests against the government will happen soon," the Señora said. "I have seen them before many times. The police fighting against the military, both fighting the people. You wait, it will happen."

"I've seen it too," Karen added, "the tear gas and the tire fires lining the streets and the highways, the guns, the police with their plastic shields." She explained further, detailing the looting and mass protests, this government only having been in power for a few months of a four-year term, armoured military vehicles bouncing down the roadways looking for aggressive protestors and perhaps hoping they find none.

We had to beat these protests, and get away before they began, I said....

We pass through the mountains, our ears plugging and then crackling clear as we go up and up, past the side of cliffs again, past their sheer edges. We suddenly stop. We are stuck in mud. The wet season is not here, just the weather leading up to it, the remnants of another storm that must have brought gusting winds and torrents of rain.

After the bus driver's lengthy struggle through the saturated earth, we are moving again. We pass by mountains of mud, sheer cliffs of it, and drive beside homes buried by landslides. We see children and their parents with buckets, emptying the dirty water from their once-proud residences. The roof of a home and the top of a palm tree protrude out of a small lake. This place has been hit hard. Someone aboard the bus says the words "*El Niño.*"

We move toward the mountains. We walk from the muddy bus station, both of us cold, and Karen dons a sweater. Removing my wrinkled and dusty rain jacket which is stuffed into my backpack, I put the jacket on and watch as the mountains fade into the evening.

The sounds of celebration, perhaps made by conspiring protestors, keep me awake throughout the night....

18

We move from the streets on the town's west side, to the countryside, by bus. We pass by a bank with people lined up outside who, as I read in this morning's newspaper, must be the patrons attempting to withdraw their savings from a bankrupt bank. The newspaper reported this to be the first in a series of events which might lead to the president being ousted. A military coup, a popular uprising, or both.

We pass by Papallacta, said to contain natural hot springs with the unique characteristic that they do not smell of sulphur. We drive throughout the night. Again, I am unable to sleep. The loud music on the bus and the occasional howling of children keep me awake during the day, and at night we are stuck in mud, either in actuality or in my dreams, which now seem so closely linked as to be the same.

Your memory is now becoming insipid and worthless, I say to myself. I barely remember the bus stopping, the planks placed beneath the wheels, the bus struggling forward on two wheels while the other tires spin in the mud. I can only recollect the flashlights, and then the heat increasing as the rising sun escalated the temperature inside the bus, which had only a few opening windows for ventilation.

Karen, still sleeping, abruptly awakens in the heat of the mid-morning air.

We drive through the sumptuous greenery of a jungle town. Abandoned muddy streets with two lampposts carry electrical power cables to the few grey buildings that need it. Tin-roofed huts are in the distance, huts with signs indicating they are for rent. There are other signs, not written in English, advertising kayaks for rent and jungle guides. I am falling into and out of sleep as, from my half-open, drowsy eyes, I see Karen rushing to the front of the bus and speaking with the driver, who slows the vehicle in the middle of this tiny town.

"We're getting off, here," she says to me after returning to her seat.

"Where is here?" I ask, sleepily.

The driver turns back toward us. "*Aquí?*"

"Here. *Aquí*," she says to the driver, gathering up our bags.

Yelena did this same thing once before, years ago, on our trip to Spain. We were in Girona, north of Barcelona along the Mediterranean coast, when she told the driver to stop. At that time, Yelena had a specific destination in mind. It was the one time I saw that she could be impulsive and adventurous, and I thought for a moment that this might be the start of a change in her. But later, after we arrived home, we discussed other locales to which we could travel. She said she did not want to go anywhere else. But at the moment when she surprised me, her sudden resolution to depart that bus seemed like a sensible idea. There was a way back, and another bus would be by within a few hours. We hiked for two miles along desolate paved roads, to reach the last workplace of Salvador Dalí, *Grafista*, Graphic Artist. The spiraling foliage, the deep blue of a Mediterranean sky, and the surreal images inside the small castle he had built for his wife still fuel my dreams.

"Why here?" I ask Karen, aware now that everyone who is awake aboard the bus is watching us inquisitively. "I know you're trying to prove something to me," I continue, "that you've changed, but you don't have to."

"Changed?" Karen asks quizzically. "Why do you say that?"

"Let's just stay on the bus until we get somewhere less remote. This town doesn't even look like a normal stop on the bus route."

"You don't think this is a normal stop, with all these signs for tourists?" she asks. And I think I can hear, at that moment, but just faintly, the words, rolling into my head in a whisper: "But anyway, neither was Girona."

We descend the stairs of the bus and arrive at the edge of a muddy street.

This place seems familiar. I pull one of my father's photographs out of my backpack and see him smiling in front of an overgrown town square, the fountain at its centre no longer functional but instead a cascade of dense foliage, the backdrop appearing to be the same as what is now before us.

"I recognize this place," I say. "At least, it looks like a town my father visited. But why are we here?"

"The Señora says this is where your father spent much of his time," she replies.

"Why?"

"He owned some huts here in Archidona, and we'll rent them from the new owner."

"I don't care to stay here, and we need to get to Quito."

"We need to rest in a bed. And don't you want to know why your father spent so much time here?"

"No, I don't."

As I try to climb the stairs to get back on the bus, its door closed now, the vehicle speeds off with a cloud of pollution. I stare for a while at the water rushing nearby, the mud-brown water of the Amazon.

After a few minutes we find ourselves unexpectedly alone in the middle of this place, without a bus in sight and without knowing when another will be coming through. I have the sudden frightening thought that the protests in the country might delay the buses, or even temporarily stop service altogether.

My anger at her, and at myself for listening to her, turns into wonderment at discovering a place that was so dear to my father. A small black monkey hops down from one of the trees within the square, noticing us, moving very cautiously at first, then scuttling away, and then returning. The animal becomes more and more emboldened after each incremental determination to discover whether or not we intend to hurt it. Staring at my backpack, which I set down, the small black-faced beast scampers toward me and grabs the pack as though it is an offering and, dragging it, unable to carry the weight, begins to examine the outside closely. It tries the zipper, slides it open, and removes a bottle of water. The monkey runs away with its newfound prize, its tail curled in anticipation as it hops up to the base of the tree, the bottle thumping to the ground heavily as it darts quickly upward.

As the sun moves behind the clouds, the image of this black monkey, who sits in the dark tree staring at us, starts to blend in to become at first dark colours, and then an absence of light.

This then transforms into the dim shade of the evening, sporadic shadows drunkenly attacking the fog of oversized insects around the two streetlights that are now illuminated. Bats are penetrating through the mist in search of their prey, before vanishing again into the blackness ... we look up for stars, which should be the most incredible array of stars we've ever seen outside our dreams. The moon is absent, and the only light for miles around seems to be from these two lamps before us, yet we can see no stars.

We step away from the lights and into a darker and more immense cloud of insects that buzz about our heads. The bugs are repulsed as we saturate our clothes and skin with a spray repellent ... the stars above remain unseen, masked by invisible clouds bringing warm rain to the already moist ground.... We have rented individual huts, to which we promptly return. The familiar sight of mosquito netting, the recognizable humming of insects, and reading several of Boccaccio's stories from *The Decameron* lulls me into sleep. I fall into a restless sleep, one devoid of dreams....

∞

The next nights are spent in the same huts, perched on stilts above the forest floor. I remember in these days and nights, as we await another bus that still has not come, what originally brought Yelena and me together. I remember our illogical conversations by having more of them, these ones with Karen. I revel with Karen in our absurdity, participating in native ceremonies by night, cleansing away any evil spirits by having a shaman breathe out healing properties through *chicha*, masticated and fermented corn juice spit at us from all angles, the shaman exhaling tobacco smoke over our aching joints and sucking and spitting out bad air, smoking unfiltered cigarettes ourselves while imagining the dark leaves to be the same tobacco as that prepared by the shaman, inventing this in our minds as we drink our own *chicha*, the natives dancing ritualistically around us in the warm rain and covered torch lights of the evening.

We marvel that we have no one to answer to here. Not each other, not even ourselves.

We are uninhibited, emancipated, free. And it is on that evening that I have the most vivid dream of my life, after I fall asleep reading *The Decameron*. It is a dream I transcribe for my therapist that, unlike Coleridge's recording of his opium-induced "Kubla Khan" dream, is not interrupted and is therefore fully articulated, in its entirety, in narrative script as the Tenth Day, Eleventh Story, as told by myself, outside of Florence in the cloudy light of day. Yelena, Karen, the Señora, Inés, Yolanda and I have all come to a hillside to escape the bubonic, pneumonic and septicemic variations of the plague which have descended upon fourteenth century Florence and taken the lives of almost half the European population.

King Gianni, ruler of Cyprus, having secretly murdered his own daughter for taking many lovers and thereby bringing shame upon him, accuses his wife's father, among others, of having played a key role in the murder. The King sentences him to death. After his execution the Queen, discovering her husband's culpability in the death not only of her father but also of their daughter, becomes committed to ending the King's life. A prognosticating witch, after declaring her allegiance to the Queen, appears to the King as an unusual black cat and prophesies that he will be destroyed. His daughter's real murderer is uncovered publicly, a war with neighbouring Armenia is lost, and the witch ensures that the prophecy comes true.

19

I AWAKEN THAT MORNING with the immediate sense that I alone am responsible for my daughter's death, and no one else. She is not dead, I reply to myself, over and over again. I quickly write down every detail and aspect of my dream, in a frenzied state that must have approached that of Coleridge as he struggled to transcribe every element he could remember. In my transcription, I leave nothing out.

While I begin contemplating the meaning of my dream, we spend our days white water rafting alone. No other tourists are here, and there are still no buses coming through. The restaurant owner says the government protestors are blocking the main highway to the nearest city, the airport city of Quito, which is four hours northwest by bus through the jungle and farther up into the mountains.

Kayaking beneath a wide-spanning bridge I not only discover that there is much of my dream which I may never analyze due to its complexity, but suddenly understand that I, in fact, was the King in my dream who had killed his own daughter.

Sitting in a restaurant without walls, just wooden poles supporting a thatch roof, barely speaking, the conversation having dwindled to that of necessity, mundane details of what we will eat, again eating muddy-tasting fish with grit that crunches in the teeth at the same restaurant, the only restaurant in the town, I realize that the liberation I felt here by covered torch lights as I participated in the native ceremonies at night—smoking unfiltered tobacco like that prepared by shamans for their rituals while drinking *chicha*, the natives dancing around us in the warm rain—was the same feeling that the King in my dream must have experienced when he burned the Queen's father beside covered torch light to conceal his own guilt.

We hike in close proximity to the hut, and then hire a jungle guide to take us to a local animal hospital, *Amazoonica*, situated on a nearby island. There we watch all but the most dangerous animals on the islands roaming free, held captive only by the water surrounding them, the spider monkeys, jungle cats and boa constrictors held in cages to prevent them from destroying the other animals.

We stand looking at an enlarged and colourful parrot with a mended wing, and I begin to comprehend that the King's daughter was killed for the sake of appearances. She was destroyed in the interests of what other people would think and of the life he had lived, and would continue to have to live, because of their talk and their gossip. I am no better than the King, who was sentenced to death. All of my own reasons for unconsciously wanting to terminate Yelena's pregnancy— the baby wasn't developing properly, the doctor said, showing us the hands and feet that were only stubs when they should have been fully developed; her heart and mind would never be right; she'll die anyway—were just meaningless justifications, the same as the public infuriation of the King where he had suspected and denounced so many when he knew himself that he was to blame. And in the end, the King was punished and died as a penalty for his crime—so, as my dream was telling me, shouldn't I suffer the same fate?

But the King was unrepentant and malicious, and I am not. That is the difference, I conclude, holding a boa constrictor, the animal nurse instructing me not to squeeze the snake when I put pressure on the animal out of fear and thoughts of my own death, shunning the realization that the King is my own unconscious self, animalistic, brutish, instinctive, visceral, without integrity and morality, the boa constrictor beginning to encapsulate and squeeze the life out of my arm as I have done.

We travel away from the island hospital in a thin and disproportionately long motored canoe, our guide accidentally letting his hand slip from the motor steering controls before quickly recovering his grip, making the boat lurch to the left. I recall screeching black monkeys and spider monkeys with immense reaches, parrots and sleek black jungle cats resembling a muscular house cat slinking through the bushes beside immense rodents the size of large dogs. Karen, facing my back in the canoe, suddenly says: "I want you to go to Venezuela with me."

"You do?" I reply. "Why? I told you I'm going back to Canada."

"It's complicated. But I really want you there with me."

I turn my head out from beneath the hood of my yellow poncho so I can better hear her voice over the sound of the motor, the light raindrops cascading onto my head and quickly wetting my hair and face as I do, and she continues.

"You didn't stay here in this country to learn more about your father, did you?"

"I suppose that, perhaps subconsciously, I did come here to share some of his same experiences, and to relive a part of my youth," I reply. "And a part of me would have wanted to come here to the rainforest, to see this place my father seemed to love so much. But it seems this was a further regression away from society for him, as it is for me. If you ask me, my father was a lot like myself, like a Gauguin without the artistic side. And even Manta wasn't remote enough for him. I'd like to have a conversation with him now, to see the state of his mind. My mother thought he was schizophrenic, one side of him wanting a social life and interaction with people, the other side wanting complete isolation, perhaps to escape from his guilt. She said that's why he came here in the first place. I'm beginning to see, from being here, that maybe she was right."

"So, without the aim of discovering more about your father, your continued presence here was from something you won't admit to, maybe not to me, or to anyone else, maybe not even to yourself.... It's not for me to say, maybe, but I think you've chosen to stay here in Ecuador for longer than you needed to as an escape from contemplating your own actions and their consequences, just as your father probably did, like a repeating pattern, or—"

"Where is all this coming from?" I interrupt, annoyed.

"I have to tell you something."

"What?"

She pauses before continuing.

"I was at the Señora's, having lunch just the other day. The phone rang and she handed me the receiver. It was your wife Yelena."

At the mention of her name, a name I have never heard Karen utter, my throat suddenly becomes dry.

"I gave her the number, in a letter, a while ago," I say. "I thought she didn't have it any more."

"Well, she does."

"And what did she say?"

"Well, she said she was somewhat relieved that you weren't there at the Señora's, actually, so she didn't have to tell you—" she pauses.

"Tell me what?" I ask, growing more impatient.

"That her baby, your baby—"

"What?"

"That it died. In a procedure. How they normally terminate a pregnancy when the mother wants—I had the feeling that she has had this procedure done before. She didn't seem as upset as perhaps she should have been, as I certainly would have been. The only explanation she offered was that she couldn't wait any more. But then again, she might have still been in shock at the realization of what she had done—"

She pauses again. I could feel my face twitching as she spoke and now I feel dizzy looking down into the muddy waters beneath our boat, the raindrops falling onto the surface and splaying out in all directions, my chest tightening with the thought that one can never lose their memory or experience, that no matter how much one tries to forget, or to run, one can never be far enough away to escape their own mind. And having read Yelena's letters over and over, which contained no talk of our child, I think now that I could have stopped her. I could have prevented this, and it would not have been difficult. Now, her actions, my actions, are irrevocable.

Karen waits for me to say something, but the wind and the unsteady hum of the motor provide the only response. We travel by large cliffs extending fifty feet out of the water and vertically upward at steep angles to end at forested rooftops with a flock of green parrots scattering overhead.

"Why did you let me come here?" I ask, turning back to face her, my tears blending in with, and washing away in, the intensifying rain. "Why didn't you tell me this before?"

"The Señora thought—actually, she voiced her opinion, as you know she has a strong opinion on everything, but really, it was me, I thought it would be better for you to come with me, not only here but to Venezuela ... so you wouldn't be alone ... and to help you to forget."

As we continue on, I recall the King in my dream, and his sentence of death. The entire kingdom was after him, including a sleek black cat with menacing yellow eyes, unnatural and not of this world, like the small jungle cat we just saw on the island, and reminiscent of the black-faced monkey we saw in the overgrown town square in Archidona. It has been prophesied, in my dream, that I shall die—

"No," I say loudly, after an indeterminate amount of time.

Karen asks if I am feeling well. I reply that I am as well as I can be, which is a blatant lie that she probably recognizes.

"My thoughts and my dreams here are too intense," I say. "I'll go back to Manta."

"No," she says, adding: "You can't escape from this. Not now. You've done enough running away alone. Stay with me. Coming with me is best."

There is a long period of silence before we arrive back on shore and then back at the huts, and I pack up all of my belongings and prepare to leave without her.

20

"THE PROTESTS ARE NOT over," the restaurant owner, jungle guide and hut owner tells me in Spanish, noticing the full backpack at my feet while he delivers a plate of fish with rice and beans. "Not yet. Still, there are no buses in or out of here, the main highway to Quito is blocked by protestors." I tell him that I have already left my rented hut, without intending to return.

"Go back to your hut," he instructs me. "There is no place else here to rent, and you have nowhere to go." He says that, as of now, there are no longer any tours available by motorized boats either, because of a lack of gasoline. Ours was the last.

I am forced back to my hut and I spend the next dreamless days and nights in solitude, sitting inside drinking *chicha* and smoking unfiltered cigarettes, eating only a single bowl of *ceviche* every day, delivered, along with cigarettes and *chicha*, by agreement with the restaurant owner, who says, when I ask, that he knew my father very well, and that, in my seclusion, I spend my time, inexplicably so in his brazenly-stated opinion, in much the same way as my father. I finish *The Decameron*. Karen knocks on my door, day after day, and I send her away, telling her that I need more time. Days turn into a week, and then two. Hearing no buses coming through town, and with no English books available here, I descend into a constant bevy of my own thoughts. I begin to paint pictures of Annabelle with some supplies I brought from Manta, and I write in a notebook that I have brought with me. All of the thoughts I transcribe are morbid. In between drawing and painting various depictions of Annabelle on the pages of the notebook, I reread some of Yelena's letters. Her voice coming through in the letters seems to have altered somehow; she seems to be speaking to me more forcibly, and with more vehemence, than ever before. All of her words now seem to be hateful accusations.

Yelena speaks about the confessions of the English Opium-Eater and how, before his addiction to drugs, he describes Ann, the first woman he had feelings for, with compassion; and how he mentions the dismal state of her life, saying how none of it is her fault, attributing her situation to the injustice of society. And when Ann disappears, an opera singer and the opium enter. The opera singer wants to introduce him to pleasures greater than the drug. The pleasures of Italian music. Rossini ... Verdi.

Looking at the ultrasound picture of Annabelle, its roughly triangular shape, the baby's outline similar to any other baby's ultrasound except to the eyes of a trained professional to whom the signs are obvious and could be, and were, explained at great length and in great detail, enough to invoke my severe nausea and which I feel sick even thinking about now, I am as Rigoletto, misled, deceived, betrayed and bent over the sack which he thinks contains the dead body of the Duke, hearing the Duke singing "La Dona e mobile" in the distance and opening the sack to find his daughter who has been stabbed and who quickly dies as Yelena joins the Duke in song.... The opera singer disappears and the next woman of interest is a servant in the house where the writer stayed. Next to enter is wine. Wine is seen as an indulgence causing him to slip into a different state of 'reality.' He is made drunk by reality and sober by the wine. The drug invigorates his self-possession whereas the wine robs him of it. Yelena elucidates the side-effects of quitting the drug and the associated nightmares, beautifully described....

Yelena tells me of her nightmares. One is recurring and involves her parents, both of them Russian Jews who are always fighting, sometimes acting stubborn and prideful like little children, traits she says she inherited. They scream at her, and she awakens shaking, with sweat and tears all over her face, but still feeling as though a terrible burden has been lifted. They were not apt to change; both of them were in their sixties and her father was having psychological and memory problems, and was lying too much, even going so far as to say he has been dying for the past several months and acknowledging that neither Yelena, nor her mother, think that is true; instead dismissing his claims by saying that everyone in the world is slowly dying. *How's your father?* I recall asking now, to which she'd reply, *Apparently, he's dying faster than the rest of us, but you would not know that if you saw him.*

One recurring nightmare she had was related to the big scars on her left leg, which extended all the way from her ankle to her thigh, scars from having been burned in a house fire when she was two years old. The nightmare took place atop a building with a lit white top, but in the dream the white top had been replaced by a huge cage with fire in it. For Laing, renowned psychoanalyst and psychiatrist, fire represented a flickering soul, I told her, a flickering sense of self. But she didn't want to hear about that, or to relive any of her nightmares through my analysis of them. She only wanted to recount them to me, to perhaps relieve herself of the encumbrance associated with keeping their memory to herself. In the dream, she went up from the ground floor in an elevator, and while she knew she was running away from someone, she didn't know who. She recalled confronting him once, though she could not identify him apart from having recognized him from other dreams. After her act of defiance she compared the sense of awe and relief upon awakening to fresh snow in the forest right after someone had skied there, those two straight lines so seamless and precise. That was how her dream was recorded in her mind, perfectly.

I continue to analyze, in great detail and at great length, the last dream I had.

I spend endless hours writing and rewriting my own eulogy, knowing that no such eulogy was likely ever delivered, or would be.

Samuel Johnson climbed down the edge of the rocks at the riverbank and entered the strong currents of the brown Amazon River, sinking into liquid that was not quite water but a dense fluid ooze with a sickly smell ... he immersed himself up to his knees, with music nearby—loud, oppressive music that would never allow one a decent night's rest—and he descended into the river, slowly, up to his waist, before immersing himself quickly; the harsh, muddy stream hitting against his face the same as the ocean water on the beach in Manta, this water also emancipating, and he could hear the sound of muted bagpipes playing as he fell into its depths. Samuel never emerged from that river, the current drawing him in toward a school of piranhas with red eyes on the hunt for flesh, their needle teeth set between frowning mouths quickly tainting the water with his blood....

(Afterword: as he was dying he thought incessantly of the daughter he had lost, and of a hotel in Madrid where he had been with Yelena ... There, on the second floor in the morning, after a long night of boozing with no sleep, he had envisioned himself jumping over the balcony and down onto the street below. He had seen his body lying there, the crowds gathering around, the hotel guests appearing at their windows, the news stories, the speculation as to possible motives, the brief instant of notoriety before the memory of his life dwindled away....)

∞

I wake up screaming into the silence and the darkness, not by virtue of a nightmare, but from a panic attack. A moment later, as a result of my scream, there are voices outside. There is pounding on my door which seems as frantic and as hurried as the beating of my heart. I long to shrivel up small enough to slip out through one of the cracks in the floorboards, to run and run away from this place and this pounding, but then I remember again where I am and what has happened. I recognize Karen's voice at the door and I tell her to go away, saying that I am well, again fully aware that I am not, claiming I need more time. She refuses to leave, saying that I should not be alone, but I am insistent, and eventually, after what might be hours, my resolve sends her and the voices away. I am again left with the sound of mosquitoes and other insects attempting to enter the netting above my bed.

The next days and evenings are spent virtually without sleep. Any amount of slumber seems to be interrupted and I rise out of bed in terror, my chest tight and my vision blurry, the room seemingly smaller than when I fell asleep. I perceive a vitriolic loss of any force or control I have when glancing over at the closed door to my hut from which I cannot escape.

One evening I awaken with a profound sense of my own powerlessness. Staring at the door in darkness as the hours pass by, I look around the room with my flashlight at the paintings and drawings I have done not only on paper but which are splayed all over the floors, the walls and the furniture, depictions of my beloved Annabelle, dozens of portrayals painted everywhere, all of the same girl with clubbed feet and shortened fingers and a diminutive head and flat face, a short neck, slanting eyes, a heart in her chest with holes exposed as if to a surgeon's knife, a rigorous compilation of images only slightly dissimilar. Thinking that her death is not her fault but due to the injustice of society, it irks and unnerves me now to see these images.

I try to breathe deeply, to relax, staring at the straw ceiling of the hut that has become so familiar to me, then looking over to the closed door, feeling the onset of panic again, looking away and trying to imagine the door open, sweating now, conceiving that Annabelle might still be alive if it was open, imagining myself knocking louder and louder on that door, pounding on the surface with my fist, my hands numb under the weight of the incessant hammering, my heart pulsating to the same rhythm as the beating, dizzy and nauseous, cursing and detesting that door for being closed and locked, longing to do anything to get to the other side of its dilapidated wooden planks, to bring Annabelle back to life.

I have the sudden, immediate and intense need to flee from this place, to wander outside, to call out for Annabelle, to run away from here with the same urgency as if it were about to be overrun by wild jungle beasts.

In an instant I grab my backpack, still packed to leave, and run outside leaving the door open behind me. Spraying on some insect repellent as I run, then producing my flashlight, I stop just long enough to put on my heaviest clothes. In the darkness, I walk near a lit area with loud, fast *merengue* music and take a long drink of *chicha*, my head suddenly cloudy with the alcohol, two additional bottles of which clink together in my backpack. Slinking off to the side to avoid a couple exiting the restaurant, where there is dancing taking place on a dirt floor, I sit down on the large rocks on the shore, in a darkened area where I cannot be seen. Stepping down further, closer to the water, I sit there and smoke one cigarette, then another, and another, while quickly and with great difficulty draining my bottle of harsh-tasting, warm *chicha*.

I sit for an hour, maybe more, watching the grey water barely visible under the moonless sky. I smoke another cigarette and descend to the level of the water. I imagine that there are piranhas here. Attacks on humans are most frequent in areas where fish are normally discarded. This is what the owner of the restaurant told me, giving me a perplexed look, when I asked.

But instead of my feet slipping beneath the surface of the river, I find they have landed on wood. I step again, and my feet both descend onto a timber surface that sloshes back and forth under my weight. A step to the left would have immersed me in water, but instead, I have landed on a boat.

I crawl into the craft and quickly discern that this was the same long, motorized canoe in which Karen and I went to *Amazoonica*, but now, the motor has been removed.

Without a thought, I retrieve a paddle left in the boat and untie the ropes that lash the vessel to shore. I begin to drift slowly into the river, contorting my body as I methodically rotate the paddle, gradually at first, and then with a more hurried, almost frantic pace into the darkness illuminated only by phosphorescent insects. With the exception of the music, I can hear only the sound of bugs buzzing around my head. I light a cigarette and they dissipate. I can feel myself sliding along the river's surface, my head murky, bewildered, my thoughts muddled, drifting with the current. Hours seem to pass, the water sloshing against the boat, the current swaying and carrying me haphazardly, the stillness accompanied by muffled music lingering like the long, drawn-out wailing of my father's bagpipes. In a moment I fall into a trance in the hurried rhythm of the *merengue* and that of the waves splashing, lapping against the shore and against the face of my impotent paddle.

As I drift further, the music begins to resonate into subdued bass tones, and as the noise fades into the distance a different music prominently emerges, one dense and replete with a thousand voices, chirrups, trills and songs, bird and animal warbles, insect calls, the Spanish voices and music now speaking indistinguishably and far off into the void as the sound of my paddle-stroking repeats. Surrounding me is an array of sounds unlike any I've ever heard, and with my flashlight I can see dense swarms of insects, thick pockets of leafy plants, a peach-coloured tree snake sitting among the branches and leaves, and I paddle farther and farther into the dense overgrowth, land and cliffs nearly indistinguishable except by the outlines on each side, my reflection in the water invisible, and darkness all around.

After an hour I remove my sweater and blanket myself with it, allowing the boat to flow with the current, trying desperately to fall into sleep; and soon, after bathing myself in bug repellant, I succumb to my exhaustion....

I dream of an empty village and huts devoid of people, and I feel that there is nothing but myself and wild beasts surrounding me. I run to find the huts are overgrown with foliage and all empty, their floors made of mud and dirt and the rocks and the forests surrounding them are devoid of life, all of the homes and the forest abandoned, and for miles around and everywhere I look I see barren emptiness with only foliage and trees, dirt and dust as my constant companions....

The next morning, I awaken to a renewed song: an overabundance of different voices, a crimson, yellow and apricot sunrise over flattened, low-hanging clouds, a tapestry above and an oil painting below in distorted, wavering reflection. A dark outline of trees separates the sunrise and its reflection, the replicated image completed in faded brushstrokes, the water rippling subtly. I am flowing backward as mosquitoes buzz about my head accompanied by the repeated, high-pitched twitter of a bird, the low, resonating call of another, the squealing and the guffaws of another, and then another, and another, all to the backdrop of the clatter of countless insects. A tree branch floats lazily by, and the mosquitoes, despite my repellant, will not let me be.

I wonder what I am doing here, floating aimlessly, and I paddle for a time as if to provide an occupation for my hands, seeing no one else except for a woman immersed in the river up to her waist, beating clothes against a rock as children play on the shore nearby. None of them notice me. I remove most of my clothing, warm in the sun now, and descend quietly into the water, slowly, tipping the canoe over on its side enough to slip into the river ... I slide in and swim, close to the canoe at first and then farther away, until the canoe is an elongated matchstick that is almost out of sight. Afraid, I quickly return and climb out of the water and back into the safety of its confines.

The day flows into night, rain beating down and then subsiding, and I experience a painful and distinct hunger. I drink from the bottles of *chicha*, from the muddy river water that grits on the teeth, and from a bucket of rainwater, in my thirst.

I become cold, my clothes damp, and the air lights up with dots of luminescence flashing in and out of vision, their radiance growing and then quickly withering away. There is a sensation of profound emptiness, the night inviting a chorus of pests and animals. I suffer through the dull ache of hunger and frequent chills. Drinking *chicha* continually for warmth, I begin to fall asleep until I notice a light on the horizon.

There is a fire up ahead, in the distance.

I immediately begin paddling toward the light, anticipating heat and warmth, and as I get closer, the noise of the bugs fades away and the fire begins to swell until, at close proximity, it consumes my view. A row of huts is ablaze, and there is a line of men passing empty and full buckets along, the men dunking the buckets into the river at one end and passing them down full, retrieving empty ones and refilling them again. At the other end, the men splash water on the huts that are quickly being consumed. It is a fruitless effort, and I am inclined to reach out and tell them.

Because I have not been sleeping well, I wonder if all of this is an illusion induced through a combination of alcohol and sleep deprivation from a lack of REM sleep, knowing that when deprived of sleep, one starts to hallucinate as though somehow dreaming by day. But this image, I convince myself, is too intense, too real.

Looking into the wavering and crackling flames, the fire producing torrents of smoke in areas where it has touched down near the wet ground, I see that on one side of the huts is a small boy, five or six years of age. He stands there, staring back at me. He has dark skin, wears plain brown clothing and has unwavering dark eyes that gaze at me as if in disbelief that I am there; as though I am some incorporeal reflection of the fire upon the surface of the water, or a vision brought on by the heat.

And in this surreal image, the sky overflowing with flame and smoke, the resonance of the boy's outline quivering in the warmth and hazy effluvium as he watches me, I have the sense that it is I who am the boy, standing there, peering back into the eyes of my father. And in that realization I can see that my father might have, in fact, been here, with his undiagnosed agoraphobia, his fear of inescapable situations the same as my own, cast out into the night alone and of his own accord as I am, as drunk as I am feeling now; and just as I have made the decision to escape from and to flee the memory of my daughter, I have already, if only subconsciously, chosen to forsake the love of the wife I can no longer love, and can no longer see or interact with, because of the life she has taken.

I watch the boy's eyes wander away from me, darting over to one side as though he has abruptly remembered another place he ought to be, or as though he is unexpectedly ashamed for having stared languidly back at this unknown stranger in the darkness, at an image that may or may not be real. As he darts away into the shadows, toward an isolated row of huts seemingly unaffected by the fire but still consumed by smoke, I am inundated by the overwhelming urge to follow. I grab my paddle and row swiftly to shore, rise out of the boat and, pulling the distended maw of the long, thin beast up onto the rocks, I run after him.

The area he had started toward, away from the men who are occupied in futilely attempting to extinguish the raging and increasing fire with small buckets of water which might as well be thimbles filled to the brim and passed daintily along, is vacant. The boy has disappeared. Looking through each of the huts that is engulfed in smoke I quickly find him inside one of them. He looks up at me and I look into his eyes again, closer this time, seeing in the shadows and fog that they are dark brown, and that he has retrieved what he came into this room, filled with diaphanous smoke, to obtain: a doll made of straw and old rags. I am barring his exit, my arms on either side of the opening, his only way out beneath my arms, and he looks at those areas of escape longingly, as though anticipating that he can dash out, scurrying away from this nonsensical man before him.

If I were to stay here for a time, continuing to block the way out in a fit of malevolence and wickedness, enough to smite the life out of this boy, my actions would not be any different from what I have done, and in fact what I have subconsciously wanted to do. I am no different from my father, or from the King in my Boccaccio dream. In the boy's gaze I see that I am again this boy looking up at my father, who chose to view me, for the purposes of his own life, as deceased; and I have the horrifying realization that I wanted my child dead, as I have just contemplated my power over this helpless child in pondering his death, the one who looks up at me now with the appearance of dread. I made it easier to end Annabelle's life by escaping my responsibilities and running away from my unborn child, I explain to this boy's stare, either in my thoughts or verbally. I made Yelena's decision easier because my absence did not preclude her actions except through a verbalized agreement, a contract that perhaps became less important and more easily justifiable to disregard over time. My father chose to have me out of his life, and as such, to have my existence relegated only to a distant and faded memory, just as Annabelle's will now irrevocably become, my father's remembrance of me interspersed with random snapshots of a boy's periodic visits, a boy left to raise himself outside of these visits in light of a mother who was never there, whose alcoholism and desire for the outward appearance of a flawless home and a perfect life seemed not only contradictory but counterintuitive. My father's kind and gentle treatment of me on my visits to Manta was a ruse of paternal compassion that I now recognize I saw him extend to any and all children he came across. And now, this boy is coughing, slumped on the floor, his eyes closing. I feel that perhaps his fear has overcome him, that he feels he cannot escape, and that he is therefore not even trying; and I see myself as following his example, lying down among these straw walls and allowing the smoke to consume my lungs and thereby extinguish my ability to breathe, giving way to what will become my end....

I feel the onset of a panic attack and I am light-headed, my feet beginning to give out beneath me, the boy perhaps beyond my ability to save him now, and in my dizziness I have a sensation of weightlessness, a slackening of tension akin to when I was floating hopelessly down the Amazon, and I am inclined to the notion that this attack will be my last, the one that will render me powerless to prevent my own imminent death. This recognition terrifies me, and I wonder if throwing myself on the blazing huts nearby, to be burned up in that fire, might be preferable; or whether slipping quietly into the water to be consumed by the river and its gluttonous piranhas would be better; and in this realization I see that I, too, have agoraphobia now and an inescapable sensation of guilt, a substitute emotion for what I am really feeling, a relentless grief and wretchedness, a lonely dejection at having run away from my unprotected and unborn child who hadn't lived, from subconsciously wanting an end to its life for which I merit an end to my own, and from having misjudged not only Yelena, but myself, so severely.

I am present here on this river, I now understand, as a consequence of my belief that I needed to suffer in order to atone for my past actions. But I must agonize in a different way by regretting such reticence and lethargy, since I can do nothing else, eventually forgiving myself and reconciling with having known that Yelena would end the life of our child, that I in fact was the King that wanted our child killed, that I was no better than my father for the pain he had inflicted upon me over the years, and that Yelena was in a closet in my recurring dream because she was hiding that my absence would give her the means by which to not only conceal her intentions, but to carry them out uncontested.

Glaring back at this boy with his now tenuous grip on my stare, as he begins to slump more and more toward the dirt floor, I have the instinctual necessity to escape from this place, to row back and to find the place called Archidona, and then Manta, from which I came.

I grab the boy by the arm, hauling him out of the hut and exposing him to the fresh air. Reviving after a few minutes, his breathing heavy and the experience inside the hut now behind us, he rises and then runs off in a mad dash toward the line of men with buckets.

Not eager to explain myself or my actions, horrified at what might have happened in the hut, at what I had allowed to happen in Canada and why, I enter the boat and begin rowing against the current, in the upstream direction I believe to be that of Archidona, with more strength, intensity and focus than ever before.

21

As THE SUN RISES over the river the following morning, having rowed through the night past bridges, tree outlines and huts that I recognized onshore, I am in awe of the splendour of this place. I see another elongated boat motoring in the distance. On board is our former guide, and Karen.

As the boat comes alongside my own, Karen jumps into the front, nearly toppling it over. The other man turns his boat around and motors away. Karen and I are suddenly left alone.

"Where have you been?" she asks angrily.

"I don't know," I say, my voice hoarse. "What are you doing out here?"

"I've been looking for you since you left. I'd nearly given up hope. I thought you'd gone mad, seeing your door wide open, and those paintings in the hut; the hut owner showed them to me, dozens of pictures painted all over the floors and the walls and the furniture, all of the same girl with clubbed feet and a small head with a flat face. To say that I was shocked, disgusted and extremely worried would only be—well, in fact, after seeing those images, I thought I'd never see you again."

"I want to travel with you," I say. "To see more of the world, to experience more than I've ever known."

She smiles after a time, and then, before we arrive on shore, she says: "The next bus will be through here tomorrow morning. The protests are long over. We have been here far too long."

22

As we travel to Quito on the morning bus, there are fires dissipating over the horizon. The fires of pacified protest. Nothing, other than this, has changed. Karen understands, without explanation, that I am going back to Manta, and not to Venezuela with her.

She leaves me an open-ended ticket she purchased for Margarita Island.

"In case you change your mind," she says, a grin on her face as she climbs aboard the bus for the airport. I call her name, and she turns around to face me.

"If not," she says, "the Señora will take good care of you. She will. Just promise me that if you're not coming to Venezuela, you'll go straight to Manta."

"I will," I say, taking her hand. "I want you to come back, soon. I want to help raise your child."

She seems confused, but still squeezes my hand as if to assure me that we will do so, together.

"I'll be back soon. This is something I have to do."

∞

Back in Manta, there seems to be a certain solemnity about the place. Inés and Yolanda are not there. The Señora tells me she is lonely. Her daughters have gone to Quito to see about their visas that will allow them to be with their father in New York.

"Karen, she will not be back," the Señora says to me in Spanish, "Unless it is many years from now. She is pregnant from a man who once lived here. Now he lives in Venezuela.

"Yes, she told me," I say, to which she appears surprised.

The Señora demands I clean every bit of paint from the walls, ceiling and furniture of my old apartment, where I have painted additional renditions of Annabelle. After I do, she hands me another key. It is the key to Karen's apartment.

"You can live there for as long as you want," the Señora says. "I told the Señorita, Karen, that your father lived in the apartment beside hers. There is a door connecting them both. You can have them both, there is no one in either. No one to rent. She suggested that you live there now. But no more painting."

"Thank you," I say. "I understand, and I won't be painting anymore."

"I will be going soon to Quito, to be with my daughters and to see about a visa for New York, for myself. You will go to Venezuela to visit Karen, and to see her baby?"

"I have the sense that she will be back here," I reply, "and much sooner than you think."

∞

The Señora asks me a few days later, in an informal proposition, whether I am interested in marrying one of her daughters and moving to New York. I reply that, although her daughters are very beautiful, I won't. I will be travelling, a short while after her return, with Karen and her child.

I carry my few possessions from my old apartment, and turn the key to the lock on my father's door. Inside, the place is the same as mine. The only difference seems to be that the roof is accessible from a pull-down ladder hidden over the kitchen, a ladder I have never seen before.

As I sit on the roof later that night smoking unfiltered tobacco, I see a spectacular array of stars. The night is cold, and the beach seems somewhat illuminated by the intensity of the stars. I can see the spot where my father is buried, and the small cross protruding from the sand....

Tomorrow, I will go down to the beach and introduce myself to the family living on the boat with the stilts, the boat that now appears as though it is floating on the water. I will not explain to them that I have intentionally littered the bay with my paintings, throwing them in the mud. I will have conversations with them about anything else. I will swim with them at the beach nearby, while watching as the tide rolls in and my paintings are washed out to sea.

I spend a few minutes writing out an alternate ending to my recurring dream.

As I fall asleep there on the roof, I again sense Yelena in the closet. I open the closet door to reveal that she is inside. She is holding Annabelle, who is asleep. Both of them are dressed in blue. "Take her," Yelena says upon seeing me, and I do. I hold Annabelle close, caressing her skin before kissing her forehead. I smell the sweetness of her skin, and I carefully remove her from the closet. I fall asleep in the dream, holding Annabelle in my arms.

The next evening I begin intentionally depriving myself of sleep, knowing that my recurring dream is over and that I will never again approach that same sensation, that same moment of overwhelming bliss, and because of that my reality, with the memory of that moment, is preferable to dreams; but I stay awake, drinking instant coffee and smoking a filterless cigarette, with the understanding that you can escape your dreams, but never for long.

QUATTRO FICTION